They reached the front entrance.

'Where's the new nurse, Jessica, living?' Andrew asked, then cursed himself as he caught Sarah's gleeful expression.

'I really don't know,' she told him, without bothering to hide her delight at his confused state. 'Perhaps in a cabin at the caravan park until she finds somewhere permanent. Helen would know, or you could ask Jessica herself.'

'Yes, well...' He couldn't put his reluctance into words.

'Don't tell me you've forgotten how to flirt,' Sarah said with a teasing smile.

'I don't want to flirt with her,' he protested, horrified by the interpretation Sarah had put on his interest. 'Although I could very well be in love,' he added ruefully.

As a person who lists her hobbies as reading, reading and reading, it was hardly suprising **Meredith Webber** fell into writing when she needed a job she could do at home. Not that anyone in the family considers it a 'real job'! She is fortunate enough to live on the Gold Coast in Queensland, Australia, as this gives her the opportunity to catch up with many other people with the same 'unreal' job when they visit the` popular tourist area.

Recent titles by the same author:

TRUST ME
AN ENTICING PROPOSAL
A HUGS-AND-KISSES FAMILY
HEART-THROB

LOVE ME

BY
MEREDITH WEBBER

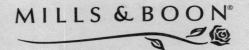
MILLS & BOON®

MILLS & BOON and MILLS & BOON with the Rose Device
are registered trademarks of the publisher.

First published in Great Britain 2000
Harlequin Mills & Boon Limited,
Eton House, 18-24 Paradise Road, Richmond, Surrey TW9 1SR

© Meredith Webber 2000

ISBN 0 263 82244 3

Set in Times Roman 10½ on 11¼ pt.
03-0006-53573

Printed and bound in Spain
by Litografia Rosés, S.A., Barcelona

CHAPTER ONE

'ABBY, I am sorry to announce this but you are no longer the woman of my dreams,' Andrew Kendall declared, bounding into the administration office at Riverview Hospital. Tall, dark blond and suntanned, his green eyes glowed with health, while his lean, fit body radiated a vitality that seemed to buzz and fizz in the air around him.

He pulled up short when he realised the object of his conversation wasn't in the room.

Then saw who was.

'Sarah? You're still here? But you're my locum! I'm back. You should be gone. Have I been sacked?'

Sarah held up her hand.

'Stop right there,' she ordered him. 'Now sit! You were always hyperactive, but to return from six weeks' leave with such energy and enthusiasm? It isn't right, Andrew. You should be tired and jaded, worn out from dissipation. Dragging yourself reluctantly back to the grindstone.'

He grinned at her.

'I like my particular grindstone. What's more, there's not a lot of dissipation to be had, climbing in the Himalayas, but it was so beautiful, Sarah. The snow-capped peaks, the pure, clean air, the people—'

'Tell me later,' she said, cutting him off before he could go into lengthy details. 'I'm staying on.'

That got his attention.

'Permanently? I *have* been sacked? Why? What did I do?'

'Stop jumping to ridiculous conclusions, cease with the questions, and listen,' Sarah told him in an exasperated tone. 'No, you haven't been sacked. I'm doing a locum for

Iain. He and Abby have been through a torrid time, she's pregnant—'

'Abby's pregnant? By all that's wonderful! Why, wait till I see Iain—'

Sarah remembered from her previous stints of working with Andrew in other country hospitals that, if you wanted to get anything said, you had to talk over him.

She tried it now.

'And she's been very ill with it,' she interrupted firmly. 'So they're taking a break. The board has arranged for a temporary nursing sister to take Helen Jackson's place on the wards and Helen's filling in as nurse-administrator while Abby's away.'

'Is the temporary sister the beauty I've just spotted in the corridor? I'm talking real beauty, Sarah. Hair like ebony silk...' He hesitated for a minute then continued with disarming honesty, 'Well, it's pulled back at the moment and looks tidy and demure, but I bet it would look like ebony silk if it were let out. Eyes as blue as Himalayan skies. Lips—well, I didn't get much of a look at her lips. Too dazzled by the eyes!'

Sarah shook her head at these raptures.

'If I were you I'd take your next holiday at a Club Med or on a cruise. Get rid of some of your physical energy in a more normal manner than climbing mountains. How long since you and Sharon split up?'

'Two and a half years,' Andrew responded, the vitality fading from his eyes. 'I came here soon afterwards.'

'And have been celibate all that time, no doubt!' Sarah guessed. 'Honestly, Andrew, you do tend to overdo things, you know! You're such an all-or-nothing man!'

He frowned crossly at her, but she ignored it, knowing Andrew's frowns were fleeting things.

'You know darned well I can't be having casual affairs with local women in a town this size,' he grumbled. 'It's too harmful to everyone. Aren't you suffering the same fate for the same reason? Honestly, Sarah, we should have got together years ago—started a nice physical relationship with no strings, no heavy stuff, involved.'

Sarah sighed. Back when Andrew had first suggested this—five years ago and, for him, pre-Sharon—she'd been tempted to agree in spite of an age difference that put him in the 'younger man' category. But she'd soon discovered she was a one-man woman—well, two-man, if you counted David.

'How did we get onto sex?' she demanded. 'There's so much else to tell you.'

Andrew smiled, his teeth a startling white against the tanned skin of his face.

'You started it,' he reminded her. 'And I'd much rather talk about sex than work. I can hear all the gossip as I do my rounds. It's always far more interesting than the bare bones of what's been happening, which is all I get in a locum's report. Even when the locum's a foxy lady with amazing green-gold eyes.'

'I thought the epitome of beauty for you was now ebony and Himalayan-sky blue?' Sarah teased.

A soft tap on the door saved Andrew answering. They both called, 'Come in.' As the door opened, Sarah realised just who had attracted Andrew's attention. Until this minute she hadn't taken much notice of the new nurse's looks, but now she checked. Yes, the eyes, set beneath a heavy fringe of black hair that all but obscured her eyebrows, *were* an unusually deep blue.

'Jessica, this is Andrew Kendall, the doctor I've been covering for. Andrew, Jessica Chapman. One of the nurses injured in the car accident before you left has decided she doesn't want to return,' Sarah explained to Andrew. 'Jessica is taking her place.'

She'd thought her introduction concise, but soon realised it was also irrelevant. Neither party had listened and, unless she was very much mistaken, she was witnessing, at first hand, an instance of love at first sight. Although she doubted Andrew would have the sense to cotton on to what was happening, and she didn't know Jessica well enough to guess what she was thinking.

Sarah coughed, making both of her companions start. Then both began to speak at once.

Jessica said in a party-polite manner, 'How do you do?' Andrew made 'welcome to Riverview' noises.

'Were you looking for me or Helen?' Sarah asked the now totally flustered young woman.

'For you, Dr Gilmour,' Jessica replied, and Sarah gave her full marks for recovery. She'd regained her composure far faster than Andrew, who was still doing his stunned-mullet impression. 'Mr Gearon's temp is up again. Sister wanted you to have a look at him.'

She turned back towards Andrew.

'Or Dr Kendall would do, I guess, if he's on duty now.'

Sarah saw the wash of heat paint pinkness on Jessica's cheeks as she spoke Andrew's name.

Definitely love at first sight.

It was going to be interesting to watch developments. What a pity she'd be spending less time at the hospital.

'We'll both go,' she decreed, as Andrew seemed incapable of a normal response. 'Mr Gearon is Iain's patient so I'll be visiting him regularly, but he'll also be under Andrew's care while he's here in the hospital.'

She stood up and gestured to Jessica to go ahead, then said, 'Andrew?' She spoke sharply enough to bring him out of his trance.

He shook his head and smiled ruefully at Sarah.

'Club Med next time,' he promised, and she chuckled as they walked towards the men's ward.

Jess used the walk to settle her nerves. This was ridiculous. Various men had paid her compliments in the past, some even swearing they were dying of love for her. One had sent flowers, candy and huge stuffed toys in an effort to impress her, yet the message she'd seen in Andrew Kendall's green eyes had said more than all those gifts and words put together.

And affected her more than any of them.

It was out of the question to even consider an attraction between them, she told herself firmly. She had a mission in Riverview, and until it was completed she needed to avoid too much personal contact with anyone, no matter what message his eyes sent.

Or the effect of that message on her nerves—which had tingled—and her heart—which had raced—and her blood—which had grown very heated all of a sudden.

Forget hot blood! an inner voice warned sternly. Think cool! Ice!

Mission!

'Mr Gearon was admitted on Saturday, complaining of a headache and of feeling very unwell,' she said, pausing in the corridor outside the men's ward and giving Dr Kendall the patient details as if he were the leader of a teaching round at a big hospital. It was easier to follow routine at times of confusion.

'Dr McPhee was concerned about meningitis and has done a lumbar puncture, taken blood for tests and done a throat swab and sputum tests. He isolated Mr Gearon in the little room at the end of Men's, although we've only got one other patient in here at the moment.'

She managed very well until she was about to explain that all the results weren't back. At that precise moment, the eyes she'd been avoiding, by looking at a tiny scar above Dr Kendall's right eyebrow, snagged her attention and she forgot Mr Gearon.

'Not all the tests results are in.' Dr Gilmour—Sarah, if Jess could only get used to calling doctors by their first names—took over. 'The cerebrospinal fluid showed a slight increase in pressure, ditto white blood cells, but as he'd been on a course of antibiotics for a throat infection that's not surprising.'

'How are you treating it?' Dr Kendall asked, and Jess, hearing his voice for only the second time, felt her body respond as if she'd known the deep, smooth cadence of it for ever.

Boy, was she in trouble if she didn't get this reaction stuff under control.

'Penicillin G, and controlling the symptoms with salicylates, and IV fluids. We've been monitoring urine output, BP, pulse and temperature hourly.'

'And nothing's shown up on the tests so far?'

He addressed Sarah, but Jess, responding to the voice, shook her head.

Dr Kendall must have seen the action, for he smiled, causing more problems under her skin, then said, 'Well, lead me to him, Nurse!'

He'd better get his mind on work as quickly as possible, Andrew decided as he followed the trim figure of the new nurse through the wide, spacious ward. Not good to be thinking of the way her body moved beneath that blue cotton uniform—although he doubted whether blue was her colour. Red perhaps?

They stopped by a bed and he reined in thoughts of colour and Nurse Whoever.

'Frank!'

He greeted his patient with surprise.

'These women called you Mr Gearon and I must admit it didn't mean a thing. Frank's the greenkeeper out at the golf club,' he explained to Sarah and—Damn, he'd been so busy re-evaluating her beauty he hadn't even listened to her name! 'What's up with you, mate?'

'You tell me, Doc, and we'll both know,' Frank replied. 'Maybe now you're back you'll sort it out.' He smiled apologetically at Sarah. 'Not that Dr Gilmour hasn't looked after me well, and Dr McPhee's taken more blood than I knew I had.'

Andrew had picked up the file and was reading as Frank spoke.

'Well, no blinding flash of intuitive brilliance has dazzled me on seeing this.' He waved the file towards the patient. 'But if all else fails we have a cute name for diseases we can't diagnose—we call it a fever of unknown origin. It lets us doctors off the hook.'

'Which, of course, should be every patient's aim in life,' Sarah added, with a teasing smile for Frank.

'What have you been up to recently?' Andrew asked, and Frank obligingly reeled off his latest work activities.

'I've put in a new green for the sixteenth, then, when it's ready, I'll pull the old one out,' he explained. 'I could never get the grass right on it.'

'And what have you used on the new one? Fertiliser? Mulch?'

Andrew was aware that both women were looking at him strangely, no doubt wondering why he was rattling on about green renovation at the golf club. There wasn't time to explain he was following the germ of an idea.

'I got hold of some mushroom compost and put that down with the sandy soil to bulk it up, then there was some old potting mix in bags in the shed so I mixed that in—'

'Legionella?' Sarah murmured. 'We did sputum tests but didn't ask the lab to do a culture for legionella.'

'Worth a try if he's used old potting mix,' Andrew told her. 'Even though, these days, it's thoroughly sterilised. I haven't heard of a case connected with it for years.'

He explained to Frank what they were going to do, while Sarah sent the new nurse—Jessica, Sarah called her—for a specimen jar.

'Should we change the drug to erythromycin?' Sarah asked as they walked away a few minutes later, the specimen having finally been obtained and the lovely Jessica dispatched to phone the lab courier to collect it. 'He had difficulty coughing up some sputum. Isn't that another indicator of legionella?'

'I'd leave him on the penicillin for the moment,' Andrew replied. 'Why did Iain isolate him?'

'We both thought meningococcal at first, mainly because he came in with red spots across his face and upper arms and chest. Then the spots faded, instead of getting worse, and it turned out they were sandfly bites.'

'Sandfly bites?'

'Allergic reaction, do you think?

'It could explain the fluctuating temperature.'

They reached the front entrance where Sarah paused.

'Well, I have to leave you with it. It's nearly nine and Iain's patients will be lining up to see his replacement. Such a disappointment for those who've already met me. By the way, I've been given permission by the board to stay on at the hospital flat. Abby offered me their house but no one else wanted the flat so I decided not to bother moving.'

'Where's the new nurse, Jessica, living?' Andrew asked, then cursed himself as he caught Sarah's gleeful expression.

'I really don't know,' she told him, without bothering to hide her delight at his confused state. 'Perhaps in a cabin at the caravan park until she finds somewhere permanent. I may have heard someone mention that option. Helen would know, or you could ask Jessica herself.'

'Yes, well…' He couldn't put his reluctance into words.

'Don't tell me you've forgotten how to flirt,' Sarah said, a teasing smile playing around the corners of her mouth.

'I don't want to flirt with her,' he protested, horrified by the interpretation Sarah had put on his interest. 'Although I could very well be in love,' he added ruefully.

'Undoubtedly,' Sarah replied, then she leaned forward and kissed him on the cheek. 'Why don't you come to dinner tonight and tell me all about it?' she added. 'Seven-thirty?'

The idea appealed, not only because he hadn't shopped but because he knew Sarah was a great cook.

'Could we make it eight? I've a late outpatients' clinic. Eight would allow me time to go home after it and freshen up.'

'Eight it is,' Sarah responded.

'I'll be there,' he promised, then turned away in time to catch a glimpse of a blue uniform disappearing into the men's ward.

Perhaps he'd better look in on Frank again.

Jess checked on Mr Gearon then sat for a while with Mr Ambrose, transferred the previous week from the city to Riverview, his home town, to recuperate from a heart by-pass operation.

'Have you had a walk this morning?' she asked him, then smiled when he grimaced at her.

'I'm far too sick to be walking, young lady!' he complained, but he let her help him to his feet, took the stick she offered him, put his free hand on her arm and began to make his slow way out to the verandah. 'Only once around,' he stipulated.

Jess didn't argue. By the time he'd been around once she was sure he would be feeling limber enough to agree to a second circuit.

'Who's that down by the roses?' he demanded, as they passed the front entrance from where they could see down to the big circular bed in the middle of the drive.

'One of the groundsmen?' Jess guessed, although she couldn't see the man clearly and wouldn't have recognised either of the groundsmen with any certainty.

'Doesn't look like anyone I've seen before,' Mr Ambrose announced, and Jess, knowing he'd spent a lot of time in hospital prior to his operation, didn't argue.

'Perhaps it's a visitor, admiring the blooms,' she suggested, but when she looked again the man had gone.

'Some no-good stealing flowers—that's my guess,' her

patient told her, leaning more heavily on her arm as
Andrew Kendall came onto the verandah through the doors
leading from the women's ward.

'So, Mr Ambrose, you're back again, but this time with
nice clean arteries.'

'I'm still a sick man,' the patient responded.

Jess tried to look noncommittal, although the smile ac-
companying the doctor's words had started her nerves tin-
gling again.

'Look at me,' her patient continued. 'A shadow of my
former self!'

'We're working on getting you a bed in the annexe,'
Andrew Kendall assured him. 'As soon as Mr Chase's
daughter can find a place for him in a nursing home near
her home in Sydney, he'll go south and you'll be moving
in.'

Jess was surprised the doctor knew about Mr Ambrose's
fear of being alone in his home, even though his chances
of another heart attack were now greatly reduced.

'Or if someone dies,' Mr Ambrose reminded the doctor.
'I'm first when that happens as well.'

Jess hid a smile. Her patient was determined to stay alive
himself, but had no compunction about wanting someone
else to die—if it meant he could move to the aged-care
facility at the back of the hospital.

'Well, we won't wish an abrupt departure from this life
on any of our friends up there,' Andrew said, turning to
Jess as if to include her in the 'our'. 'And don't fret about
going home. I'll keep you here as long as possible. Judging
by the lack of occupied beds, the air around the town must
be exceptionally healthy at the moment.'

He fell in beside them, and as they walked slowly along
towards the kitchen he talked to the older man about his
holiday.

It sounded fascinating, climbing in the mountains, but
Jess found it hard to concentrate on his descriptive account.

His voice was one distraction, but Mr Ambrose's remark about someone from the annexe dying proved an even more effective mental block.

Not yet! she prayed. Not yet.

It was the beginning of a long and tantalising week for Andrew. Long because of a waiting list of minor surgery that had him operating most days on top of his usual hospital duties. Tantalising because Jessica Chapman was working in the same environment, and sending waves of disturbance as potent as nuclear radiation through the air around him.

She wasn't doing it deliberately. He'd realised that almost immediately. She was friendly, co-operative, a kind and empathetic nurse from what he'd seen of her, but as elusive as mist as far as getting to know her better was concerned.

'Have you seen much of the area around Riverview?' he asked on the Wednesday, when he had her cornered in the dispensary.

She looked startled for an instant then shook her head, which didn't surprise him as he'd already learned she used gestures with her speech.

'Not a lot,' she said politely—she was always polite as well—then she ducked past him and disappeared, but not before he'd seen a flash of apprehension in her eyes.

Which left him feeling both puzzled and slightly guilty.

'Do you think she's hiding some great sorrow?' he asked Sarah later. 'That there's something hidden behind her polite, determinedly cheerful and utterly beautiful façade?'

Sarah sighed.

'We're talking Jessica, I assume. Why don't you ask her, not me? Or make a date with her? Get it over and done with.'

'I tried,' he said gloomily, then realised he hadn't really

tried but had merely skirted around the issue like a bum-
bling youth.

He gathered himself together, practised what he had to
say and made another attempt on Thursday when he caught
her in Men's, helping Mr Ambrose on with his slippers.

'Are you on duty over the weekend?' he began.

She glanced up from where she squatted on the floor and
smiled her lovely smile.

'Yes,' she said.

He was stumped, so certain he'd been on a winner this
time.

'Oh, that's a shame,' he muttered, and stalked out of the
ward.

'Maybe the trouble's with you, not her,' Sarah suggested
when he repeated this second abortive effort to secure a
date. 'Has it occurred to you you're going about it the
wrong way?'

'With Jessica, I've a feeling any way will be the wrong
way. I mean, look at me, Sarah. I'm fit, not that bad looking, have a good job and no attachments. You might not
believe this, but there are nurses in this hospital who have
all but thrown themselves at me.'

'But not Jessica,' Sarah said with a smile. 'Did you consider she might not be interested in a workplace relationship? Any relationship at all, in fact? Maybe there's someone special back in the city.'

'Then why would she come here? Why leave that special
someone?'

Sarah chuckled at his intensity.

'Hey, I haven't done too good a job of my own love life,
remember? I'm certainly not qualified to sort out someone
else's.' She paused then added, 'But maybe she had a reason to come here. I was thinking about what you said yes-
terday, and I agree. There's a deep reserve behind that
cheery smile and gentle manner. She might take some getting to know, your Jessica.'

'My Jessica?' he repeated gloomily. 'She's a long way from being that.'

Jessica was off duty on Friday and Andrew missed her, missed the anticipatory feeling that any minute he might walk through a door and see her. And over the weekend, although he spent more time than usual at the hospital, all the staff were busy with minor injuries and accidents. There was no time for social chat or abortive invitations.

'Dinner again tomorrow night?' Sarah asked him when she ran into him outside Outpatients on Sunday evening.

'Better than having no social life at all, I guess!' he muttered.

'Well, that's a backhander!' Sarah said, and he caught her arm and kissed her apologetically on the cheek.

'I'm sorry. I've sent Frank Gearon home without ever really knowing what was wrong with him. Mr Ambrose has been bugging me about the annexe—'

'And you haven't won the lovely lady.' Sarah added to his list of moans in the same gloom-encrusted tone he'd been using.

'Barely laid eyes on her all day,' he confirmed, then he brightened because he enjoyed Sarah's company and did need some relaxation. 'Dinner tomorrow night would be lovely. Eight o'clock again?'

CHAPTER TWO

THE outpatients clinic finished early on Monday evening, so Andrew drove home, showered and changed, then decided to walk back to the hospital for dinner with Sarah. His body felt fit and supple after the exercise in Nepal and he was determined to keep it that way.

He strode effortlessly along the quiet streets of the town, then out along the path that ran beside the river. The occasional splash of a fish jumping and the soft rustle of a night creature in the grass were the only sounds, the river flowing silently, its power controlled, contained within the banks.

He left the path reluctantly, climbing the grassy bank when he guessed he was directly opposite the hospital. He'd misjudged, but not by much. He was opposite the entrance to the caravan park, which was set in spacious grounds a few hundred yards from the hospital.

He crossed the road to gain the footpath and it was then he saw the figure standing under the single streetlight that provided ineffectual illumination between the hospital and the park entrance.

And recognised the midnight dark hair, loose around slim shoulders, dishevelled in a way that made him feel uneasy.

'Jessica? Are you OK?'

He moved closer, instinct telling him to take her in his arms but something in the way she stood warning him to wait.

She looked up at him, her eyes huge and frightened in her tense, white face.

'Which way did you come?' she asked, the words so shaky he barely made them out.

'From town.' He nodded in that direction. 'Along the river path. Has something—someone—frightened you?'

He put out his hand and saw her flinch, so he drew back again.

'It was probably nothing,' she said lamely, her voice stronger now and colour returning to her full, soft lips. 'A noise. I looked behind me and didn't see anyone, but with the trees…in the dark… I came to the light and—'

'It could have been a small animal of some kind,' Andrew suggested. 'I've been hearing them myself, but you've had a bad fright, whatever it was. Treat for shock, that's the first thing. I'd put my arms around you just to warm you up, but that might upset you more. Look, I'm going to Sarah's for dinner. Why don't you come? She'll have enough for three. I don't think you should be on your own until your nerves have had a chance to settle down.'

None of which sounded very medically correct, he realised, but the urge to hold her close until her fear went away was so strong he was pulled towards her, while the vibes she was giving off, telling him to stand back, warned against it.

'We'll walk up there together, and if you don't feel up to dinner I'll get you a warm drink in the kitchen then walk you home again. Damn it all, what a night to not have a car! I could borrow Sarah's. Drive you home.'

He watched her closely as he made these suggestions, and was relieved to see the tension leaving the tendons in her neck and the look of strain lessening in her eyes.

'Or Sarah could drive you home,' he added. Although that wasn't his favoured option, it might make Jessica feel easier. The level of fright suggested Jess had had a bad experience—no doubt with a man—some time in the past. 'Come on. Back to the hospital.'

She turned obediently and began to walk beside him, but he knew from the way she carried herself that the fear lingered.

Could he take her mind off it for a while? Get her talking? Personally, he'd rather have walked in silence, listening for any sound that might indicate a hidden presence, his eyes alert for moving shadows in the dense shrubbery.

He opted for conversation. For her sake.

'You're out late. Were you working a split shift?'

She shook her head and the inky waterfall of hair, loose for the first time since he'd met her, swayed silkily.

'I'm new here, and although the staff have all been very kind and welcoming I don't…' She hesitated, then changed tack. 'I like to take my time and get to know people before getting overly friendly. Besides, I'm used to being on my own.'

Again she paused, and Andrew wondered what she'd been going to say originally—before that hesitation. Not that he didn't believe the eventual explanation, but the sentence hadn't hung together neatly.

'I go over to the annexe most afternoons after work,' she explained, as they turned into the hospital grounds. 'I don't work there, but sometimes I help feed one of the less able residents, or join a game of cards, or take someone on at snakes and ladders. Old Bob's a demon at snakes and ladders.'

Her voice was steadier now, but her shoulders were still held too stiffly back for her to be completely relaxed.

Perhaps she, too, was listening and looking.

'Bob's a demon in a lot of ways,' Andrew agreed, to keep the conversation flowing. 'He starts an argument just to stir things up.'

This brought a soft chuckle and a slight relaxation of those tense shoulders.

'Don't I know it,' she agreed, but she didn't elucidate. She was looking around quite openly now, as if to reassure herself she was safe.

'Well, what's it to be? The hospital kitchen or Sarah's flat?' He was surprised by how badly he wanted her to choose the latter, although dinner with a colleague wouldn't normally be an ideal choice for a first date.

'I can't intrude on Dr Gilmour,' his companion protested, but without much force. They had reached the bottom of the steps leading up to the front entrance and paused while she made her decision.

'She'd be delighted. Besides, she's a woman. She'll know exactly how to tackle the possibility of someone hanging around the hospital at night. And if you come to dinner I can see you home afterwards. Tuck you safely into bed!'

It was the sudden stiffening of those shoulders again that told him his last joking remark had been a mistake.

He touched her lightly on the shoulder.

'It was a figure of speech, Jessica,' he said gently. 'I won't now, or ever, intrude into your life, your personal space, without a specific invitation. Is that OK?'

She gazed up at him, her eyes dark shadows in the dim light shining down from the verandah, her clear brow furrowed by a puzzled frown.

'Why would you want to?' she asked, her voice more uncertain than unsteady this time.

He smiled, and hoped she'd see reassurance in it.

'You're a very beautiful woman,' he said lightly. 'Is it so unlikely an unmarried, very eligible bachelor with absolutely no unsavoury household habits should be interested in you?'

He saw the doubt in her eyes change to tentative wonder, and the smile trembled then settled more firmly on her lips. Then, as quickly as the joy had come, it dimmed, and she shrugged.

'I guess,' she said, but what she guessed he couldn't tell because she'd walked on, leaving him to find some consolation in the fact that she was heading towards the hospital flat, rather than the kitchen.

Don't get involved, Jessica reminded herself. You're here for one reason and one reason only.

She set aside the thought of where getting involved had led before—that was the past. Behind her.

All but forgotten.

Until she'd heard a small animal rustling in the grass beside the path and freaked out! Made a fool of herself in front of Andrew Kendall.

'Hey! Slow up. We won't get into trouble if we're late.'

His voice tugged at her nerves and sent little shivers down her spine. All this from a command to slow down?

She chuckled at the idea and turned to face him—catching again the messages in his clear green eyes. Were her eyes reflecting them? Giving back signals she didn't want him to have?

'Oh, there you are, Andrew! I was beginning to think you'd been waylaid. And you've brought Jessica with you. How nice.'

Jess felt her cheeks heat with embarrassment, although Sarah couldn't have sounded more welcoming.

'I'm sorry. I didn't want to intrude but—' How to explain she was too frightened to be alone—even in the hospital kitchen, with people buzzing in and out?

'She had a scare,' Andrew explained, ushering both her and Sarah inside. 'Noises in the bushes. Have you heard any reports of anyone hanging around the hospital lately?'

Sarah shook her head in reply, then put her arm around Jess and drew her towards an old armchair.

'How terrible,' she said. 'Here, sit down. I'll get you a drink. Something hot or cold? What do you think, Andrew? I've got some brandy.'

Jess found comfort in the woman's touch, but shook her head at the offer of brandy.

'I'd probably pass out and, really, I'm all right now. It was probably as Dr Kendall said—a small animal making noises in the bushes.'

'Dr Kendall?' Sarah echoed. 'Haven't I told you it's first names here at Riverview? Call him Andrew or no one will know who you're talking about.'

Jess looked doubtfully at the man in question.

Andrew? Could she call him Andrew and still keep him at arm's length?

'Andrew!' the subject of her thoughts said firmly. 'Nothing else, you hear?'

Sarah, who'd bustled away after delivering her edict on names, returned with a glass of pale amber liquid.

'It's a very small brandy, with lime and soda. Makes the brandy palatable and it certainly isn't enough alcohol to affect you in any way. Just a steadier—doctor's orders.'

She handed the glass to Jess, who took it and sipped obediently.

'A light beer for you, Andrew?' Sarah asked.

'Nothing right now, thanks. But if your dinner won't spoil with waiting a little longer, I might pop across to the hospital and check on a couple of patients before we eat.'

Something in his voice alerted Jessica and she looked up from her drink in time to see an unspoken message pass between the two doctors. What it said, she had no idea— although other unspoken messages had been very clear.

With Sarah's blessing on a further delay, Andrew crossed swiftly to the hospital where he collected the big torch kept just inside Cas. Long strides took him to the front gate, then he slowed as he reached the footpath, shining the light into the tangle of bushes and trees that grew beyond the fenced boundary of the road.

It was impossible to tell if someone had been there, the torchlight not strong enough to pick up crushed grass or broken branches. He wondered about the mentality of someone who'd lurk in the bushes, waiting for an unwary female to walk that way alone.

Although how many of the hospital staff would walk home at the end of a shift?

Did anyone walk anywhere these days?

He reached the entrance to the caravan park and realised that the thick band of vegetation he'd just searched was part of the park property. Trees and bushes had been planted along the front fence, no doubt to beautify the place and possibly to keep out traffic noise and fumes. Perhaps a dog had been snuffling through the undergrowth, or some innocent park resident had taken a stroll beside the trees.

He walked back, thinking of seeing Jessica again—and enjoying Sarah's dinner. The idea of a lurker was dismissed.

He was sorry Jessica had been distressed by the incident but pleased it had given him a chance to get to know her a little better, even if she hadn't exactly welcomed his brash expression of interest in her.

He returned to the flat to find Sarah hadn't dismissed the incident quite as lightly.

'Come and help me serve,' she suggested, then led him into the small kitchen. 'I haven't said anything to Jessica because I don't want to add to her alarm, but I will speak to Helen about it. It might be as well if everyone keeps an eye out for strangers in the area and perhaps we could have a groundsman or orderly in the car park at the end of the evening shift just in case some unsavoury character is hanging around.'

'You're taking this seriously?' Andrew asked.

'You bet I am,' Sarah told him. 'I've been working with Jessica for a couple of weeks now. She's efficient, level-headed and sensible. In my opinion she's not a woman who'd frighten easily.'

Efficient. Level-headed. Sensible.

The words conjured up lace-up shoes and a determined jaw, perhaps glasses, and definitely a firm, no-nonsense set of lips.

Not the beauty who sat, sipping at her fortifying drink, in Sarah's living room.

'How were your patients?' that same beauty asked as he set two meals on the little dining table and indicated they were ready to eat.

It took him a moment to process the enquiry because she'd smiled as she'd spoken and sent his mind off at a tangent.

'Fine,' he managed to reply, while Sarah, entering in time to catch the conversation, grinned at him. He considered his options and decided it was better not to pursue the lie so he changed the subject.

'I spoke to Frank Gearon earlier today. Phoned him to check if he's had any recurrence of the headaches. He's feeling fit and healthy again but keeps asking what was wrong with him.'

'Very awkward, that,' Sarah agreed. 'Patients do like to know. They want a disease or illness named so they can tell their friends they've had such-and-such.'

'It could have been an allergy with Mr Gearon,' Jessica suggested as they took their places at the table. 'I mean, he'd had the throat infection and was on antibiotics before the headaches started, but then he was attacked by the sand-flies. If he got them all at once—perhaps usually used a lotion to keep them at bay then forgot to put it on one day because he wasn't feeling well—'

'Have you been sitting there thinking about hospital patients since I left the room?' Andrew asked, and saw a swift rush of tell-tale colour stain her cheeks again.

'Not all the time,' she admitted, her blue eyes twinkling into his in such a beguiling way his heart lost its beat and faltered before resuming proper work again. 'Sarah and I were also discussing men!'

'Men, or one man in particular?'

He tried to make the question sound casual, but from the look of feminine delight on both their faces he hadn't succeeded.

'Oh, one man!' Sarah said lightly, then she grinned at Jessica.

'Mr Ambrose!' Jessica delivered the punchline of their silly joke, and Andrew told himself he'd known all along they were teasing.

'He's paranoid about going home,' Sarah said, the talk turning serious now. 'Jessica was saying she thought you'd picked up on that as soon as you returned. Was he very fearful before he had the bypass?'

'Terrified!' Andrew confirmed, realising medical topics were safest given the newness of this love-sickness he was suffering. 'No amount of counselling, no personal alarm or regular roster of visitors, could convince him he wouldn't have a second heart attack and die before help arrived.'

'Did he go home, or did you send him straight from the hospital here to the one in the city?' Sarah asked, waving her hand to indicate they should start eating.

'We sent him home but wangled funds for a carer for a fortnight,' Andrew told her, then he tried the meal, a lightly spiced curry. 'This is delicious, Sarah.'

He ate some more while he thought back to that time, the months before his trip.

'After that his daughter came to stay with him for a few weeks, and by that time he'd reached the top of the list for the bypass and we could pack him off. We've got him booked into the annexe. He's old enough to qualify but he can't go in until there's a room available.'

'Which is why he's probably plotting murder as we speak,' Jessica said. 'He's very put out that someone won't die to let him in, so perhaps that's his only option.'

Andrew chuckled.

'How do you think he'd do it? I mean, an explosion or a spot of arson wouldn't work because he'd be destroying his prospective residence. Poison? Save up a few of his drugs then dissolve them in someone's cocoa?'

'He'd have to know what drugs killed and what didn't,'

Sarah pointed out. 'What about strangling someone with their dressing-gown cord?'

'But if it looked like murder, wouldn't he run the risk of getting caught?' Jessica objected, getting into the spirit of things. 'Then he'd end up in jail instead of the annexe.'

'Well, at least he'd have people watching over him there, ready to call the ambulance if he had a heart attack.' Sarah pointed out the safety factor and they all laughed. Andrew noticed that Jessica was relaxing, a more natural colour making her pale, clear skin look healthy again, the glow in her eyes defeating the stressed look.

'So it would have to be something made to look like an accident,' he suggested. If the macabre conversation was helping Jessica over her fright then he'd see it continued. 'Something easy even an old and fairly frail man could manage.'

'Smothering?' Jessica suggested. 'A pillow across the face. Would that work?'

'Or what about an air embolism?' Sarah said. 'I've always thought that would be a good way to murder someone. Picture our villain, dressing-gown flapping, hypodermic in hand, creeping down the corridor towards his chosen victim's room! He pushes open the door, slides towards the bed and strikes!'

Andrew laughed but thought he saw Jessica shiver and wondered if perhaps they'd pushed the joke too far.

'Wouldn't he have to find a vein or artery?' Jessica asked, sounding interested enough for him to think he might have imagined the shiver. 'I mean, to get an air bubble into the blood?'

'Don't spoil the plot with practicalities,' Sarah told her. 'I was trying to think of an undetectable method.'

'Poison's the go,' Andrew said. 'It's a favourite in murder mysteries and it's always put into curries so the victim doesn't taste the bitterness.' He grabbed his throat and made a dreadful gurgling noise, stopping only when Sarah began to slap at him with her napkin.

'I think we should change the subject,' she suggested after she'd made him promise to behave. 'Apart from anything else, Jessica's had one fright tonight—she doesn't want any more. Tell us about your trip.'

He was glad to oblige, explaining the economics of the country that now relied so heavily on tourism and the beauty of the mountains through which he'd walked.

Both women prompted him from time to time, but it was the wonder in Jessica's eyes that spurred him on and made him ask, much later, as they were washing the dishes while Sarah made coffee, 'Have you travelled much yourself?'

She shook her head, and again his gaze marvelled at the movement of that dark curtain of hair.

'I will one day,' she said, so positively he wondered if she'd already made the plans. He felt obscurely upset to think it might be so. Then she added almost under her breath, 'One day!' He felt better, certain it was still a dream, not a plan.

'OK, children, coffee in the lounge then you can both go home,' Sarah decreed. 'At my age I need all the beauty sleep I can get.'

'At your age!' Jessica repeated. 'You're what? Thirty-two, thirty-three at the most?'

Sarah chuckled.

'You're a dear girl, and I love you for the compliment, but I'll have you know I've a daughter of nineteen. I'm heading for forty so fast I can't bear to think about it.'

'A daughter of nineteen?' Jessica repeated. 'I didn't realise you were married.'

There was an infinitesimal silence, then she added, 'Oh! What a stupid thing to say. I'm sorry, Sarah, I'm usually not that crass. After all, it's how I grew up—just me and Mum.'

Andrew heard the pain in Jessica's voice and caught the confusion in Sarah's eyes.

'How is your Lucy, by the way?' he asked Sarah, deftly steering the conversation onto another new track.

'Second year at university in Armidale and blooming,' Sarah replied. 'She absolutely loves it. Stays in college but has plenty of friends to escape to when the meals get too predictable or she feels she needs a change.'

Jess willed away the sudden sadness her own indiscreet comment had brought flooding back. She blinked back tears and swallowed hard. It was emotional stress, she told herself while Sarah listed the subjects her daughter was studying.

Plus the fright she'd had earlier.

'Ready to go?'

Andrew's voice broke into the lecture she was delivering to herself.

'Of course,' she responded, getting to her feet and turning to face Sarah. 'Thank you so much for having me,' she said. 'I'm sorry to have interrupted your plans.'

Sarah smiled, then, to Jess's surprise, stepped towards her and gave her a warm hug. 'If it had been my daughter who'd had a scare, I hope someone would have taken her in and fed her. I'm just glad you're feeling better now.' She turned to Andrew. 'You'll see Jessica right home, won't you?'

Andrew nodded, then kissed Sarah lightly on the cheek as he added his thanks for the meal and hospitality. It was a peck, nothing more, but Jess sensed a familiarity between them and felt a sharp stab of what couldn't possibly have been jealousy.

'Where are you living?' Andrew asked, when the farewells were completed and the two of them were walking down the drive.

'In a cabin in the caravan park.' Jess told him. 'I booked in there before I came to town, thinking it would give me a base while I got my bearings, but it's so comfy I think I might stay on. It's handy for work as well. I don't have a car.'

'Don't have a car?' Andrew repeated, as if the idea were as bizarre as having three legs or two heads. 'Can you drive? Do you have a licence?'

Jess shrugged, then decided attack was the best form of defence. 'Hey, I've lived in a city all my life. Parking a car is far more trouble than using public transport.'

'Granted,' Andrew said, stepping behind her so he was between her and the bushes now they were beyond the hospital grounds. 'But you're in the country now. In this area most kids are steering cars around the paddocks as soon as they're tall enough to see over the wheel.'

They'd reached the entrance to the caravan park, and Jess was suddenly reluctant for the evening to end.

'Well, that didn't happen with this kid,' she told him, pausing outside the main gate. 'And I must admit, I've never felt the need to learn. I mean, once I have a licence people will expect me to drive. I have friends who go out with their boyfriends or partners and always have to drive home.'

'And you, Jessica?' Andrew asked. 'Is there a boyfriend or a partner who would have liked you to drive him home?'

He spoke softly, but the words seemed to burn into her skin. She understood why he was asking, knew he was expressing an interest in her, but she had no idea how to handle it.

'No,' she said, realising honesty was important. She was about to add that she intended to keep it that way when he smiled in response to her answer and her brain stopped working altogether.

'Come on. I promised Sarah I'd see you to your door,' he said, taking her elbow and steering her down the drive. 'Where do we go?'

'It's down here. The last cabin on the left,' she managed

to explain, battling against the weakening effects of his touch and the seductive power of his tall, lean body walking so close to hers.

'This one? Bloody hell!' The oath erupted so hard on the heels of his question that Jess was stunned.

'What? What's wrong with it?' she asked, but Andrew wasn't going to answer. He dropped his hold on her elbow and raced around the back of the cabin, making such a racket as he crashed through the undergrowth that she realised the noises she'd heard earlier probably had been those of a small animal.

He reappeared at the other end of the van, his shirt untucked on one side, his longish, sun-streaked hair dishevelled.

Without explaining his peculiar behaviour, he hustled her over to the door, demanded the key, unlocked the cabin, then urged her inside and snapped on the light. His grip, which had tightened on her elbow, now slackened and he turned, held her shoulders and eased her down onto a seat in the little dinette.

'I don't want to frighten you, but there was someone out there near the cabin. He or she ran off as we approached, but right now I'm going to see the park manager and ask him to have a look around, then I'm going back to the hospital to get Sarah's car. You will lock the door behind me, then pack. I won't be long, but don't open the door to anyone but me. Understand?'

Jess shook her head.

'Not one bit of it,' she told him, although fear now sneaked into her confusion. 'And why am I packing? I'm all for the park manager having a look around, and I'll keep my door locked, but I'm not letting anyone frighten me away.'

Her companion didn't answer immediately, but knelt in front of her and took her hands in his. He looked up at her.

'You've been frightened twice tonight,' he said, his voice

very serious but still uniquely appealing to her ears. 'It might be coincidence, just someone being a nuisance. But you could also be a target, and that's not a nice idea.'

'A target?'

Andrew looked into those sapphire eyes and realised he didn't want to see more fear in them. Why bring up stalkers? Worry her unnecessarily?

'Because you're a woman living on your own,' he said. 'Easier to scare than someone who has friends or family around them. That's why you're packing.'

'Yes?' she prompted, which was just as well as the feel of her small slim fingers in his had Andrew's mind wandering off on a tangent.

'You can come and stay at my place,' he said firmly. 'Three-bedroom house in the centre of town, nosy neighbours both sides. Just until this is sorted out.'

Wariness made her eyes seem even larger, and he felt the fingers try to slide away from his grasp. He held on tighter and spoke quickly.

'I meant what I said earlier about not intruding in your life, Jessica. You'll stay as a friend and colleague, nothing more.' *No matter how my body feels about it!* 'Do you want a pledge on that? A solemn oath?'

She smiled and his heart stopped working again. Damn thing! It was like a car overdue for a service.

'I'm sure I can trust you,' she said, her simple faith in him more effective in ensuring a hands-off policy than any promises of his own would have been. 'But I hate to put you out like that, and I'm not sure it's necessary. I was frightened earlier, but—'

'But nothing—you're coming with me and that's that,' he cut in before she could raise any more objections. 'And we'll arrange things so you get a lift to and from work. In fact, if we ask Helen to fiddle a little with your shift times, you could travel back and forth with me. Perhaps visit your friends at the annexe when I have an early evening session, or before work if you're starting late.'

Andrew watched her face. He was absurdly anxious for her to agree with his plan, although the non-intrusion clause would make it hard for him to pursue his interest in her.

He tried to guess what Jess was thinking, but her eyes were fixed on some internal problem, their blueness reflecting back the light but not the workings of her mind. He sensed a wariness in her and wondered again about her past.

And why so lovely a young woman should be unattached.

Had she recently broken up with someone? Would that explain the reserve she hid behind her smile? The move to the country for a self-confessed city girl?

Stalkers were often rejected suitors.

The thought was so unwelcome his fingers tightened involuntarily on hers, and he felt her flinch as if he'd hurt her.

'Please agree, if only for my peace of mind,' he said, releasing her hands and standing up. 'Come for tonight— a few days—enough time for the local police to increase patrols in this area, check if there is anyone hanging around.'

She nodded, but her eyes held apprehension as well as wariness.

He smiled encouragingly, then wondered fleetingly what the lips that half returned the smile would taste like. Pulled himself together sufficiently to repeat his order about locking the door, promised to be back as soon as possible and departed before he could talk himself into believing that the hands-off policy didn't begin until she was his guest.

CHAPTER THREE

JESS packed.

Staying with Andrew Kendall might not be the best idea in the world, but he'd infused enough of his concern into her for her nerves to be twitching with more than his physical appeal.

And *that* was going to be tricky—no matter what promises he'd made about not intruding into her personal space. The way her body was behaving, he didn't have to intrude. Being anywhere within half a mile of him could cause problems.

She paused midway through folding her second uniform into her suitcase.

She shouldn't go! Shouldn't risk the distraction of living as well as working with the man she found so attractive.

But if she didn't move to his place, would she be able to stay on at the annexe after work—visit the old folk, get closer to them? To the one she sought to know?

Or would she be too afraid to walk that dark path on her own? Would she always see shadows moving as she approached her cabin after dark?

She finished folding the uniform and put it in the case, then heard Rob Walsh, the manager, call to her as he walked behind her cabin. She went to the bathroom and grabbed her toiletries and towel. If living with Andrew Kendall was the only way she could complete her mission, she'd just have to learn to ignore incidental things like eyes the colour of clearest jade and the beguiling way strands of gold-streaked hair flopped across his forehead.

The possessor of these attractions knocked on the door and identified himself as she was trying to find a description for a mouth full-lipped but not too full, a smile that combined charm with warmth and understanding.

'Are you ready?' he called.

She unlocked the door and pulled it open, studying her visitor as the light spilled onto him. There wasn't really a description to fit that mouth—except perhaps perfect.

Or tempting.

She licked her own, suddenly dry lips and answered him. 'Two minutes.'

He was about to step up into the cabin when he paused, then bent low, muttering under his breath, 'What's this?'

He straightened up with 'this' in his hands—a tired, drooping rosebud of deep, velvety red.

Jess shivered, realising he'd been right earlier—someone had been near her cabin.

'There's a note,' Andrew said, raising the wilted flower to the light. 'Dreadful handwriting, your intruder.'

He frowned at the small piece of cardboard tied to the stem, and Jess guessed he was trying to make light of it for her sake because his voice suggested more anger than humour.

'Well, if it's any consolation, it's not addressed to you but to someone called Kristie, whom he loves.'

While Jess tried to absorb this new information, Andrew pulled a handkerchief from his pocket and wrapped both rose and note in it.

'Are you packed?' he asked, when he'd tucked the parcel into his pocket.

She stared at him, emotional overload making it difficult to understand the words.

'You'll be OK,' he promised, then he stepped up into the cabin and, ignoring the agreement established between them, put his arm around her and gave her a quick hug.

Its effect was like a tonic, wiping away the fear—or pushing it so far to one side she no longer felt its icicles in her blood.

His touch fed warmth into her body, and comfort, and companionship—not to mention weird ideas she was better off not having.

Not right now.

'Ah, you're almost ready,' he said, taking in the scene with one all-encompassing glance.

He removed his arm and stepped aside, putting space between them again. She took the hint and folded a jacket she'd considered leaving out. The suitcase was already over-full, yet everything had fitted in when she'd moved to Riverview.

'Clothes expand when left out in the open,' Andrew said, stepping in behind her and surveying the small mountain rising above the case's sides. 'It's one of life's laws. Would you like me to hold the lid down while you zip it up?'

He was so close she could hear him breathing, imagined her ears had picked up heartbeats as well—but those could be her own.

'If you wouldn't mind,' she said politely, although she was so wound up from the way he'd held her and then stepped back that she wanted to yell at him. For what, she wasn't certain.

They closed the case between them, their hands springing back when they accidentally brushed.

This is definitely not a good idea, Jess's inner voice warned, but Andrew had already carried her case out of the door and was putting it into the boot of Sarah's car.

He turned back to ask, 'Is that it? Surely you've got more? Or are you only passing through? Temporarily here?'

'I travel light,' she said, hoping he'd drop the subject. Not that she owned much more than the suitcase full of linen and clothes. It, and two tea-chests of belongings parked in a friend's garage, was the sum total of her worldly goods and chattels.

Refusing to be depressed by the thought, she found her

handbag, slung it over her shoulder, then grabbed a small cardboard box, which she'd kept because she hadn't found a paper recycling bin as yet, and packed her meagre supply of groceries into it.

Andrew returned and lifted the box from her hands, peering into it. 'Is this all the food you have? It's a good thing you're moving in with me and not me with you. A man could starve to death!'

She knew the comment had been light-hearted banter rather than a reflection on her housekeeping, but the trauma of the evening had caught up with her.

'I buy food as I need it,' she retorted. 'Don't worry, I'll feed myself at your place. I won't be a burden to you.'

He smiled, defusing her anger and letting the magnetic fascination back into the void.

'You could never be a burden to me,' he said quietly.

Jess glanced at him, then quickly looked away. Her body had reacted to the messages she'd seen earlier, but her mind was reminding her that even silent messages counted as intrusion and she should be pointing this out to him, not shivering with delight.

She looked around the cabin to take her mind off such rampant folly.

'I should clean the bathroom, sweep the floor,' she said. 'I can't just walk out and leave the place dirty.'

'It looks clean enough to me,' Andrew told her. 'Anyway, Rob told me you'd paid a month in advance and still had a couple of weeks of that time to run. Come back when you're off duty if you really want to clean. I might even help.'

He was teasing her, which was nice, she decided, then remembered she didn't want him being nice to her.

She remembered something else.

'But if I'm paying rent for the cabin here, I can't afford to pay you board as well. Nurses' wages don't cover such extravagances.'

She'd turned towards him to make her objections so she saw Andrew's eyes darken and the perfect mouth firm.

'I am inviting you to stay with me, which makes you a guest,' he said in a voice that told her arguing would be futile. 'Guests do not pay board or rent or anything else.'

She opened her mouth to argue but he held up his hand.

'You may contribute to the groceries, as long as you promise you won't spend all my hard-earned money on the healthy-looking stuff you have in this box. I'm all for sensible eating, but muesli? Uncooked porridge, that's all it is!'

He grumbled his way out to the car. Jess locked the door and followed. If she could control her physical responses to this man, and work out some financial arrangement that didn't bankrupt her but eased her conscience about accepting his hospitality, then living with him might be fun.

Emotionally risky, of course, but still fun.

Fun? The word kept recurring in her mind.

Having fun? What a concept! Would she remember how? When had she last really had fun?

'It will work out just fine,' Andrew said, and she realised he must have been watching her approach—and reading her thoughts, from the sound of his voice. 'We'll have fun.'

Definitely reading her thoughts.

She climbed into the car.

Andrew drove slowly home, talking about the town, its history as the centre for a rich pastoral area and the decline many country towns had suffered as transport became faster and cheaper.

'Have you always worked in country towns?' Jess asked.

'Always,' he said, with more conviction than she'd expected. 'I'm a country boy, born and bred. You can have your city, Jessica. Give me the wide skies, the clean air, the birds and trees and smell of just-cut grass.'

She smiled at the images his words drew in her mind.

'I can understand that part, but isn't country practice limiting? Don't you ever feel you'd like to be doing more?'

She was talking to make conversation, but as he pulled into a driveway and the headlights illuminated an old stone cottage she forgot the questions and exclaimed, 'But it's beautiful!'

A low chuckle rumbled from his throat.

'Did you expect me to live in a hovel? Or perhaps in a very modern brick and tile duplex?'

He cut the engine as he spoke, and the sudden silence seemed to hang between them.

'I hadn't *expected* anything,' she admitted. 'But the garden—hollyhocks at the front door, it's so perfect.'

'You can thank Abby McPhee for them,' Andrew told her. 'For all the garden. The house was a mess, and I've been concentrating on renovating it. Abby's been living in a rented place, so she used all her gardening energy on this place.'

There was silence while they both contemplated the result.

'It's called a cottage garden,' he added, and Jess detected more than a hint of pride in his voice.

'Perfect for a cottage,' she said softly.

He touched her lightly on the shoulder, then switched off the lights, plunging them into darkness.

'Well, let's get you settled in,' Andrew said, launching himself out of the car so swiftly she wondered if she'd said the wrong thing.

She followed more slowly, carrying the box of groceries, waiting until he turned on lights before venturing inside.

The stone walls were so clean she guessed he'd stripped either layers of paint or some kind of cladding off them in his restoration work. In the lamplight, they glowed a pinkish gold, perhaps reflecting back the gold of the polished floorboards.

'It's beautiful,' she said again, guessing he'd prefer the simple to the superlative in praise.

'It has come up well,' he admitted, glancing around then leading the way upstairs. 'Bedroom's up here.'

She followed him and passed a small bathroom on the top landing, then entered a bedroom with windows shaped to fit under the eaves and a view towards the eastern hills.

'There are clean sheets on the bed. I keep it made up for visitors. You get a good sunrise from here,' he told her, 'if ever you're awake to see one. My bedroom gets the sunset—something that occurs at a far more civilised hour of the day, although I'm rarely here to see it either.'

He dropped the suitcase and backed out.

'You passed the bathroom, and the kitchen's downstairs. Make yourself at home. Perhaps when you've unpacked, had a wash or shower or whatever, you'd like to come down and have a cup of something. We could talk about your roster, and how we can make our schedules fit.'

Andrew escaped, feeling far worse than he had at fifteen when he'd asked Shelley Ryan to go to the school formal with him.

It wasn't as if he hadn't had women live with him before, although not for a while—and not like this. Not platonically.

He made his way slowly down the stairs.

It was a bit rough on a bloke when, for the first time in two and a half years, he really wanted a non-platonic relationship with a woman, and he'd promised her it wouldn't happen.

It was a matter of willpower, he decided, pacing the bright rug in the middle of his living-room floor. And attitude.

If he treated her as a friend—a mate, a colleague—surely he'd stop thinking about sex every time he looked at her.

Satisfied that this was the answer, he made his way to the kitchen where he put milk in a pot and set it over a low gas flame to heat. He searched his cupboards for some Ovaltine left from a young cousin's visit. That should help his guest sleep.

The problem was, he realised a little later when she came tentatively into the kitchen, wearing a long straight garment in a blue that rivalled her eyes, he'd never had a mate who made his heartbeat falter, or whose appearance tied his guts in knots and made him want to pant like a very thirsty dog.

'I—I've made Ovaltine,' he managed to stutter, at the same time wondering why he'd rejected blue as her colour and ever pictured her in red. That deep dark blue turned her skin a pearly, almost translucent white, like the heirloom fine bone china his mother collected and treasured. It also enhanced the colour of her eyes so they shone like stars in a clear night sky.

'I haven't had Ovaltine since I was a child,' Jess said, taking the mug he offered and wrapping her hands around it to absorb its warmth.

'Bring it into the living room. I've put biscuits out in there, although whether chocolate TimTams are what should follow a curry dinner, I'm not sure.'

He knew he was talking for the sake of it, making conversation to stop himself saying something he might regret, moving away from her in case his hands escaped the control he was having trouble exerting and reached out to touch her.

She followed him into the living room, went unerringly to the chair he didn't use and settled into it, curling her bare feet up under the skirt of the long dress.

'I'm on an eight-to-four shift all this week,' she said, 'but there's no need for you to bother about giving me a lift. I'll enjoy the walk, and I can still visit the annexe and leave early enough to get to the town before dark.'

He waved away her objection.

'I'm up there most of the time myself. Even on golf days I do a round after I finish playing—that's Wednesday and

Friday, by the way, so you can stay on later with your friends in the annexe. Monday I have a late outpatients clinic, but the other days I'm free to leave at any time you're ready. And an eight o'clock start is good for me as well.'

Why was he sitting here discussing timetables when what he wanted to talk about was the way her hair fell in such shining beauty to her shoulders, and how come light seemed to shine through her skin?

Because he'd promised, he reminded himself.

No, he hadn't, his inner devil reminded him.

But she trusts you, the good guy countered.

And won.

'For a few days we'll drive,' he said, returning to time-tables as a safer topic than shiny hair. 'Rob was going to phone the local police. Have them come out in the morning and take a look around. In all good detective stories, people lurking in bushes leave cigarette butts.'

He spoke lightly and was rewarded with a glowing smile, then she sobered and said, 'I'm not sure if finding some-thing will make it better or worse. I mean, it would reassure me that I hadn't overreacted to the noises I heard, but it would also raise a whole lot more concerns. Like who. And why.'

Damn! Why had he brought the subject up again? The light in her eyes had gone out, and she was looking small and apprehensive again.

'Hey, don't worry about it now,' he said. 'Unless there's a lunatic boyfriend in your past who might have followed you to Riverview.'

He was joking, but the sudden tensing of her shoulders told him she hadn't found it funny.

'He wouldn't have followed me to Riverview,' she said, her voice so tightly strained he could feel it cut across his skin, 'and most people who know him would refute the lunatic tag.'

'But he frightened you?' Andrew prompted, knowing enough psychology to realise it was better talked about now he'd inadvertently raised the subject. She smiled at him, but it was a sad shadow of the smiles he'd seen earlier.

'He frightened me,' she admitted, 'but not physically— well, in some ways physically. He phoned all the time— after I broke it off—at all hours of the day and night. Called around to my house. It was his...' She faltered then went on. 'His intensity! It was so all or nothing!'

Andrew heard the echo of the words Sarah had used about himself the previous week, and shuddered.

Then his guest's smile brightened slightly as she added, 'It left me very little personal space, which, I guess, is why I'm wary now.'

'Well, he sounds exactly like the type who'd turn into a stalker,' Andrew said, recovering well considering she'd just reminded him, not so subtly, of his promise. 'I can get Rowan, the chap in charge of our constabulary, to check him out for you. Make sure he hasn't pulled up roots and followed you to Riverview.'

This time the smile positively shone.

'I don't think that will be necessary,' she told him. 'Heads of surgery at major city hospitals very rarely transfer to country towns and, anyway, I doubt his wife and children would like being transshipped. That was something else that bothered me about him—finding out he'd lied about a separation.'

Andrew swallowed the expletive which had sprung to his lips and marvelled that his house guest could look so composed, considering what the rat fink had done to her.

He'd find out who—easy if he discovered where she'd worked before Riverview—and some day track the blighter down and tell him exactly what he thought of him.

For now, he'd better find a new topic of conversation, although the anger he'd felt was still being manifested in tight bands around his chest, and his mind was more on revenge than conversational subjects.

'It's in the past,' his visitor said, taking the initiative from him, 'and, I must admit, he was very kind to me when my mother died. I probably leaned on him more than I should have, and gave him a false impression as well.'

The bands tightened and the urge to maim this unknown man grew stronger. The wretch had taken advantage of Jess when she'd been emotionally vulnerable. Well, he'd show her that not all men were like that. That a man could be a kind supportive friend and not demand payment in bed—or wherever the bloody surgeon had demanded payment.

'Did your mother die suddenly?' he asked gently, putting thoughts of Jess in bed right out of his mind.

The shiny hair fell forward as she nodded.

'An aneurism. One minute she was there, the next she was gone. It happened at her work, so quickly it took a little time to—to accept.'

Andrew felt his gut wrench, with sympathy this time, and realised he was going from bad to worse with these conversations they were having. She'd said at Sarah's that she had no father, so she must be all alone in the world. Now she'd go to bed and cry herself to sleep, thinking of her mother. Could he somehow get back to neutral ground?

'Is that why you left the city? Went bush? Because of your mother's death?'

She shrugged, hesitated and finally made a decision to respond, nodding as she answered.

'Yes!'

Then she lifted the cup to her lips and drained the last of the drink from it.

'I'll just wash this out then go to bed,' she told him in a voice that held sorrow but no tears. 'It's been a long day, one way and another.'

Jess walked away, pleased she'd been able to talk about her mother without crying but mortified that she'd told

Andrew so much about her life. It was as if it had all been sitting there, waiting to come out—like the insects in Pandora's box.

He'd shown a modicum of sympathy—played the polite host—and she'd practically given him chapter and verse of her abortive affair with Robert, not to mention her mother's death.

Oh, Mum!

The words rang in her head as she rinsed the cup, yet they didn't prompt tears. Instead, an inner peace came over her, as if she'd just received a very special blessing. She hugged it to her, this sense that her mother was close, and took its comfort with her as she left the kitchen.

'Goodnight, Andrew,' she said, almost gaily, as she passed through the living room again on her way to the stairs. 'And thank you for everything.'

His eyes met hers, and she felt her smile fading, inner peace not enough to withstand physical responses. What was it about this man that could make her body react with such vigorous abandon?

'Goodnight, house mate!' he said, his voice so gruff she wondered if he was reinforcing her position in his house for himself, rather than for her. 'Sleep well!'

She did, waking only when the sun shone directly on her face, its warmth making her turn away until she realised what had woken her.

A glance at her watch had her leaping out of bed, and she scowled at the mountains that had kept the sun hidden until seven-thirty.

'Bathroom's empty!'

Andrew's voice reminded her of the previous night's excitement, while her inner self recalled other sensations and sent them twitching through her nerve fibres.

'Thanks,' she called in answer, but from the sound of his footsteps on the stairs he'd already gone too far to hear her.

Grabbing a towel and clean underwear, she headed for the bathroom, then realised she was in someone else's house and couldn't wander around half-naked. She found her clean uniform—she'd have to talk to him about washing—and took it with her as well.

Ten minutes later she was in the kitchen, surveying an array of breakfast cereal Andrew had lined up on the kitchen bench.

'Do you eat a little of each?' she asked, finding her own muesli and pouring some into a bowl.

He shook his head.

'It's a shopping problem rather than a taste matter,' he explained. 'I often think I'd like a change, so when I'm shopping I buy something different. Then I try it, and don't like it as much as what I had the previous week, so...'

He seemed so genuinely puzzled by this aspect of his character she had to smile.

'We might take cereal off the list of groceries we buy out of combined funds. Looks like it would cost you a fortune to keep up this selection.'

He grinned at her and lifted a coffeepot.

'Coffee? Or do you prefer tea?'

'Coffee if it tastes as good as it smells,' Jess told him, and, although she meant it, she realised the words were just that—words. Underneath them, something else was going on. Something she couldn't quite understand, and didn't really want to explore.

It was like radar, silent signals transmitted through the ether, entering her body and stirring up revolt.

They ate, the polite veneer of conversation continuing, while his body bombarded hers with wordless messages.

'OK, let's roll,' he said. 'Do you do teeth again?'

She smiled at him, surprised at how domestic it sounded to be discussing teeth-cleaning with a virtual stranger.

'After coffee, yes,' she told him. 'I'll only be a minute.'

She was halfway up the stairs when she remembered something else.

'You've got Sarah's car. What about your own? I can't drive it.'

'Don't panic,' he said, then smiled in such a way it made her nerves flutter. 'We can walk home from work—or, if it seems too far, get a lift.'

Too far?

She repeated the words as she cleaned her teeth.

She'd already gone too far, agreeing to move in with him.

'Perhaps the police will catch whoever it was today, then I can go back to the cabin,' she said, as she followed Andrew out of the door and into the beautiful sunlit garden.

'And leave all this?' he teased, turning in time to catch the look of wonder on her face.

'It *is* beautiful,' she murmured. 'My mother loved this type of garden. Apparently, where she grew up, everything was planted in rows and nothing was allowed to spoil the symmetry of the grounds.'

This time she had to blink away a tear and, when Andrew took her hand to help her into the car, she didn't snatch it back, but drew comfort from its warmth and its silent message of support.

'So, where are you working today?' Andrew asked, settling behind the wheel and backing carefully out of the drive.

He saw his house guest smile as he changed gear and headed down the street.

'In with the men again,' she told him, 'but as there are so few patients I'm also covering Outpatients and Cas. You'll be sick of the sight of me by this evening.'

'I doubt that,' he said politely, but fate was certainly against him. For maximum control he needed minimum time with her—that much he'd decided late last night when he'd peered in through her bedroom door to check she was OK. For the sixth time!

'Rowan Crane, the policeman I mentioned, is coming up to the hospital at nine. I'll explain to Helen what happened. He'll want to see you.'

He'd have preferred not to have brought her fears back to the forefront of her mind, but a large policeman appearing without warning in front of her might have caused even more consternation.

'I'll be there as well,' he added, then hid a wry smile. As if she needed him! This woman had survived her mother's death, as well as one of the hierarchy where she'd worked making a nuisance of himself. She was tougher than her bone-china figurine appearance suggested.

'I'd appreciate that,' she said softly.

He turned towards her, realised she meant it and immediately felt about two feet taller!

She's a mate, he reminded himself as he pulled into the hospital entrance then drove on to park in the carport attached to the hospital flat.

He turned to say 'See you later', as he would to a mate, but realised his passenger was already out of the car, heading back towards the gate. He was considering this action when she turned and came rushing back, bending low to peer into the car.

'The rose,' she said urgently. 'Have you still got the rose? I didn't look at it too closely, but when we passed the big rose-bed I thought perhaps...'

She stopped and he watched embarrassment give colour to her cheeks.

'It was probably a stupid idea,' she finished lamely.

'It isn't a stupid idea but a brainwave,' he assured her, getting out of the car so they could talk without Jessica bent double. 'I dropped the rose and note in to the police station last night after you'd gone to bed, but we'll suggest

Rowan checks the rose garden for a match when he comes later.'

'Good morning, you two!'

Sarah appeared, and Andrew was pleased to see her wrap her arms around Jessica and give her a big hug.

'You're having a rough time, aren't you?' Sarah said to the younger woman. 'But you'll be safe with Andrew!'

And over Jessica's dark head, Sarah shot him a 'she'd better be' look!

'As if!' he muttered at Sarah, then he walked away, redundant now as either a protector or a comforter.

CHAPTER FOUR

REDUNDANT also in Cas a little later when a child with a discharge from the right ear was brought in.

'He didn't complain at all,' Jane Simmonds told Andrew, indicating two-year-old Peter who was sitting happily on Jessica's knee. 'It wasn't until I noticed the stains on the pillowcase I realised there was something wrong.'

'Have you mopped out infant ears before?' he'd asked Jess, who'd seen the patient first and then had found Andrew in Women's a few minutes ago.

'Once or twice,' she'd admitted. 'I spent my last few months at St James in Cas.'

As far away from the surgeon as possible! Andrew had guessed as they'd walked together back towards the examination rooms.

Now he'd prescribed antibiotics and had suggested a regular mopping operation, and knew he could leave it all to the nurse.

If he wanted to.

Or if he had something urgent awaiting him elsewhere.

'Come on, little man,' Jessica was saying to the child. 'We'll get some of this gunk out of your ear.'

Peter looked entranced—well, what bearer of a Y chromosome wouldn't? Jessica settled the child between her legs and tipped his head so that his left ear rested on her knee and his right, infected ear faced upwards.

Holding a cotton bud very lightly in the fingers of one hand, she gently eased the pinna back and down to allow access without hurting the child.

Six soiled sticks hit the basin before she was satisfied,

then she released the child and picked him up, kissing him soundly on the cheek.

'That's for being a very good boy,' she told him. 'Do you want to go back to Mummy now?'

His little body snuggled closer to Jess, then he turned and held out his arms towards his mother.

Andrew felt his heart go into erratic mode again, and wondered why he should be affected by the sight of two women and a child.

Or had it been the one woman?

The image of the child in her arms—of motherhood?

He was trying to rationalise his confusion when he realised Jane was hovering and Jessica was asking him something.

'I wondered how many times a day you wanted the ear mopped out. It's probably easier for Mrs Simmonds to bring Peter up to Outpatients than to do it herself.'

He was sure Jessica's words made perfect sense and that it was he who had the problem, but for some reason they took a long time to translate to meaning in his head.

Perhaps because the idea of motherhood had suggested fatherhood—a really terrifying prospect for a bachelor.

'Three times should do it—perhaps after lunch and again late this afternoon or early this evening. Before Peter goes to bed. Tomorrow, come in the morning again.' He was addressing Jane now. 'By then the antibiotics should be taking effect and we'll know it if needs continuing attention.'

'If you live in town, I could come to the house this evening. It would save you bringing Peter out,' Jessica offered.

Andrew felt aggrieved by this suggestion and realised it was because his house guest was making plans that didn't include him.

Yeah, right! So now you think you own her! That's exactly what she doesn't want!

He said goodbye to Jane and Peter, and escaped before

he grew even more confused. He found himself back in Women's before he realised he'd written nothing on the patient chart.

Jessica was doing it for him, her head bent and one corner of her bottom lip teased at by two white teeth. Her hair, as always when she was working, was tied neatly at the nape of her neck, so he saw her classic profile and again considered the similarity to a china figurine.

Except a figurine wouldn't colour so delightfully when it realised it was being observed.

'Would you say the discharge was watery?' she asked. 'Do you want those details on his chart? I've put down it took six cotton buds and that it was slightly bloodstained. It doesn't smell.'

Once again it took a moment to get his brain into the right gear for playing doctor.

'Watery,' he answered. 'Are you always this thorough? What options were we taught? I remember purulent or bloodstained, odourless or offensive—there was a third, wasn't there?'

She looked up from the chart and grinned at him, then ticked off the answer on her fingers.

'The type of discharge, its nature—ropy or watery—and odour. I had to read up on my paediatrics when I was transferred. That's the only reason it's still fresh in my mind.'

The woman was kind, as well as having a wonderful grin, he decided.

He watched her cross the room and add coloured buttons to the sleeve of Peter's file, before slipping it into a drawer in the filing cabinet.

Efficient, too.

And what had Sarah called her? Level-headed? Sensible? Stunningly beautiful!

Although those were his words, not Sarah's.

'There's no one waiting for us in either Cas or

Outpatients, so perhaps we should go through to Admin. Isn't your policeman due?'

Once again the lovely Jessica had taken the initiative and startled Andrew out of a most uncustomary daze.

He nodded numbly and stood aside so she could precede him from the room.

It was because of the hands-off business, he excused himself. Knowing she was off limits, which had built up a kind of mystery in his head, making her seem even more appealing—intriguing—challenging!

And thinking about mystery, there was Rowan striding up the front steps.

Andrew stepped forward to Jessica's side, and introduced her to Rowan, Rowan to her. The policeman's not-so-subtle appraisal of Jessica's beauty had Andrew quietly gnashing his teeth, and understanding why some Muslims covered their women's faces with yashmaks.

She's not your woman! common sense reminded him, but as Rowan ushered Jessica into the admin office Andrew found it hard to believe common sense when his body was asserting something entirely different.

'Well, we've a six-year-old Kristie in year one at the school and another of high-school age, but she's away at boarding school so I guess that's not the one your note-leaver meant. There's no Kristie on the electoral roll and, as far as I can find out, no one with that name has just moved here or is living here on a temporary basis.'

Rowan was gruffly reassuring, but from the look on Jess's face it hadn't worked.

'I was hoping someone at the caravan park...'

'I've checked everyone there—not a Kristie among them. Not surprising, really, when most of the residents are older people. Apparently it wasn't such a popular name fifty or sixty years ago.'

Rowan explained this to all of them, Helen included, then turned to Jessica.

'I don't suppose it's your second name or a nickname?'
She shook her head.

'It's a mystery to me, but I must admit I feel slightly better knowing whoever it is out there chose me by mistake. I suppose that's wrong of me but, although I'm sorry for Kristie—whoever she may be—I'm really glad he's in love with her, not me.'

'If it's a mistake, perhaps it's because you look like someone,' Rowan suggested. 'I don't suppose you have a double?'

Jessica chuckled at his hopeful question.

'Not that I've ever met.'

'Abby said you reminded her of someone, but I don't know that she ever worked out who,' Helen put in, peering closely at Jessica as if to find a likeness that might not exist.

'Do you know where Abby and Iain have gone?' Rowan asked. 'Perhaps if we contacted her, we could ask if she knows a Kristie.'

'Don't look at me,' Andrew said. 'They'd gone before I came back. Helen?'

Helen shook her head.

'All I know is Queensland!' she said. 'They headed north to find sun and beaches. Decided they'd stop at the first place that appealed to them, but that could be anywhere.'

Rowan sighed. 'I suppose if it becomes any more serious, I can get the Queensland police to find them, but right now it's probably more important that Abby has a good rest.'

'Jessica thinks the rose may have come from the hospital garden,' Andrew told him, realising it was the only clue they had. 'Did you bring it with you?'

Rowan shook his head, his eyes once again on Jess.

'No, but I can bring it back. Perhaps you could walk around the garden with me,' he suggested to the nurse. 'Identify the right plant.'

Purdah was also a good idea, Andrew decided, and carefully restrained himself from offering to accompany them. Everyone in town knew his thumbs were red, not green.

'Is that all?' he said instead, wanting Rowan out of there.

'Not quite,' the policeman answered, and his eyes grew grave as he looked from Jess to Andrew then back to Jess again. 'There *were* signs that someone has been in the band of vegetation along the caravan park fence recently—twigs snapped off, grass trodden underfoot where a person has waited. Around the back of your cabin is the same, although, as both Andrew and Bob went charging through there, it's hard to say what's what.'

He turned to Helen.

'I think you have to warn the staff to look out for strangers, and to be careful when they're outside at night—walk to their cars in pairs, take sensible precautions.'

Helen shuddered.

'I hate this kind of upheaval,' she complained. 'It sets everyone on edge—but you're right, they should be warned.' She glanced at Andrew. 'What about Jessica? Are you happy for her to stay with you? Jess, does that suit you?'

Andrew nodded and waited for Jessica—Jess—to respond. He tried the name in his head and found he quite liked the diminutive.

'I feel it's an imposition on Andrew, but I don't want to make more trouble for anyone, so I'll stay there until it's sorted out,' she said, speaking to Helen, but knowing he'd understand the limit she was imposing was for him.

'That's great,' Rowan said. 'And in the meantime we'll keep looking, maybe find a Kristie and get the perpetrator that way.'

He thanked Helen for her time, said goodbye to Andrew and Jessica and departed.

'What a nuisance!' Helen muttered, then, as Jessica flinched, she looked up and smiled. 'Not you, Jess. You're the victim here. It's absolutely dreadful for you. My problem is that I'm a better nurse than I am an administrator, and I hate having to deal with anything out of the ordinary. For instance…' she looked at Andrew '…because the police are involved, should I report this to the board? Do you know?'

Andrew considered it.

'I'd include it in your regular report. When do they meet? Next week?'

'The week after,' Helen told him. 'And, yes, I think you're right. We'll handle it in-house but tell them about it later.'

She waved a hand towards the door to dismiss them both, then pulled a sheaf of paperwork towards her with a martyred sigh.

'Take care of that girl,' she said as Andrew followed Jess out of the room. 'I've lost enough nurses lately.'

'Does offering you coffee come under the heading of taking care of you?' he said to Jess.

She turned and smiled.

'Only if you explain to Sister why I'm not back on duty in Men's.'

She whisked away and he was left in the corridor, his mind a tangled mass of unrelated thoughts, his body besieged by frustration.

Which built and built to volcanic proportions over the following days. Jessica was the perfect house guest, polite, helpful, even cooking the evening meal one night. But she was remote, removed, the ties he'd felt between them from that first meeting tugging them together but her coolness, her control—and trust—holding him at bay.

'So, who was the lucky recipient of your visit this evening?' he asked, as they drove home on Wednesday evening after he'd built up frustration of a different kind at golf, then returned to the hospital for a ward round and to collect his visitor.

'Mrs Cochrane.'

The name was softly spoken, as if Mrs Cochrane was somehow special to her.

'Well, if you're getting on with her you'd charm a snake,' Andrew said. 'She's an old tartar.'

'She's a lonely old woman,' Jess argued, her heart aching as she realised how true that was. 'And in spite of her frailty, she's mentally very acute. Fascinating, if you can get her talking.'

'All her own fault she's lonely, from what I hear,' Andrew said crisply, 'although you're right. She's good value when you get her going. She knows more about the history of this area than anyone I've ever met.'

'Yes, she's happy to talk about that,' Jess agreed, and wondered how long it might take to get Mrs Cochrane off the town's history and onto her own life.

For ever?

'Not keen on history?' Andrew teased, and she smiled at him, aware of how easy it would be to fall in love with this kind, undemanding man who seemed to sense what she was thinking and feeling, then fit right in with it.

No way! she reminded herself.

'Not that keen,' she admitted. 'So, how was your day? Your golf game? I was working on the women's ward this morning. Did young Peter come in again or is his ear better?'

Andrew didn't answer immediately and she wondered if he'd guessed she'd changed the subject deliberately. Now she was getting closer to Mrs Cochrane she wanted to hug the little bits of information she was gleaning to herself, not talk about them.

Definitely not talk about them.

'Peter's ear is better, although he'll have to finish the antibiotics. My golf was lousy, the day not much better, its only bright spot being the drive home from the hospital.'

They were pulling into the yard as he spoke and he turned to her as the car slid to a stop.

'And the drive there wasn't half-bad either,' he added, smiling in the way that made her blood thicken and her pulse pound in her ears.

'That's a very pretty compliment, but we have an agreement, remember?'

Her heart was beating so erratically she had trouble speaking, but she knew she had to play it cool, to act as if he had absolutely no effect on her, no matter how her internal bits and pieces were behaving.

'I said I wouldn't intrude until I was invited,' he reminded her. 'But everything about you is an invitation.'

The words were like a soft wind playing on her skin, bringing nerve endings to attention, anxious to relay messages to her heart and lungs.

Use your head, not your heart and lungs, she told herself, but when he followed the words with the lightest of touches, his fingertips stealing up her arm, across her neck, tilting her chin so she had to look into his eyes...

'I won't intrude,' he said in a whisper, then he made a lie of the promise, bending forward and brushing a kiss across her lips, the touch petal soft, butterfly fleeting.

He sat back and she knew it was up to her to make the next move, wanted nothing more than to lean against him and kiss him in return.

Playing with fire, Jess! her head warned.

Are you ready for what will surely follow?

'So, what's for dinner tonight?' she said, her voice shaking so much he probably guessed the effort she was making to not kiss him back.

'My turn to cook,' he said, and his voice was as strained as hers had been shaky. 'Do you eat pasta? Fish? I do a great pasta marinara, using whatever seafood I happen to have secreted in the freezer.'

'That sounds wonderful,' Jess told him, then realised that

they were still sitting in the car, held there by the strength of the unfinished business between them.

Would just one kiss be so dangerous?

Yes!

She opened the car door but was still reluctant to move, so in the end Andrew alighted first, crossing to the corner of the cottage where he turned on the tap to get his sprinkler system working in the garden.

Perhaps she'd imagined the power holding them together in the confines of the car.

She got out and walked to the front door, reluctant to use the key he'd given her.

Thinking of keys, and how at home—domesticated— Andrew looked, bent over some bright lupins as he adjusted the spray on one of the sprinklers. Not thinking of where she walked. Not looking.

The roses were soft and squishy under her foot and, assuming it to be an animal of some kind, she shrieked and leapt back.

Andrew was by her side in seconds, so it was he who knelt and lifted the mutilated blooms.

'Damn him to hell!' he roared, and flung the flowers into the garden.

'Shouldn't we give them to Rowan?' Jess was so shaken the question came out like a whimper of fear.

'Yes, of course we should,' Andrew said savagely, putting his arm around her shaking shoulders and drawing her close to his hard, warm body. 'But he can damn well come and get them. I'm not leaving you alone, understand?'

He unlocked the door and hustled her inside, then turned her in his arms and held her for a minute until both their pulse rates had settled slightly and she could no longer hear the air going in and out of either of their lungs.

'Was there a message?' she asked, easing away from him as other signals began transmission through her skin.

'I didn't look,' he admitted, releasing her and stepping

back then running his fingers through his hair. 'Didn't think, which was stupid of me.'

'Your reaction felt just right to me,' Jess told him, and saw his surprise, and the sudden glow of attraction light his eyes.

'Tread carefully, my lady,' he warned, 'if you're not ready to issue invitations. And speaking of invitations, I'd better phone Rowan then go out and find the evidence.'

There was a moment of silence, then he said, 'Are you OK?'

Jess nodded, unable to speak, although the emotion clogging her throat was gratitude for this man, not fear of the unknown one.

Not that the fear remained at bay for long. Rowan brought it home to her with a few simple sentences.

'He didn't need to leave a note. The flowers themselves are the message. He's left them to show he knows where you are,' he said, arriving in response to Andrew's call a little later.

'Great!' Andrew muttered. 'And so we know he's still around. Surely there can't be a stranger in a town this size for long without someone knowing about it. I mean, he must be staying somewhere. And Jess has only been here a fortnight herself, so you'd assume it was someone who arrived within that time frame.'

He glared at Rowan, who was being remarkably ineffectual about all this.

'We've checked,' Rowan said. 'There's no one at the pub—a few backpackers coming through on the Oz Experience bus but that's all. And none of them have stayed for any length of time—all moving on within the week. Rob hasn't any new lodgers at the caravan park and local gossip can't place anyone turning up in town and finding a bed with a friend or relative.'

'Well, ghosts don't go around leaving flowers on doorsteps,' Andrew fumed, aware he was far too worked up about this to think logically.

'What about neighbours?' Jessica suggested. 'Perhaps someone saw a stranger around the place. I would imagine a man walking down the road with a bunch of roses would be noticed in Riverview.'

'Of course,' Andrew agreed, although he hadn't realised his brain was working *that* slowly!

'I'll be asking around,' Rowan promised, then he stood up. 'Well, I'd better go. Keep in touch.'

Andrew walked him to the door, but he'd noticed Jessica shiver and he saw Rowan out with more speed than politeness, returning to hold the fearful woman in his arms again.

'Rowan doesn't think he'll go away, does he?' she whispered. 'That's what his "keep in touch" meant, isn't it?'

She murmured the words against his shirt as he ran his hands up and down her back, soothing her as he would a nervous animal.

'Not necessarily,' he temporised. 'He's just letting us know he's there for us.'

'Us?' she repeated, and he tightened his hold on her slim body.

'Of course "us", Nurse Chapman. We're in this together, you and I.'

He sealed the promise with a quick kiss on the top of her shiny black hair, then remembered other promises, including one to make dinner, and released her reluctantly.

The drama had unsettled both of them, Andrew realised, so he suggested they eat dinner in front of the TV to anaesthetise themselves. Not the best idea from another point of view, considering the spatial limitations of a two-seater lounge.

Yet it was good in one way. He could see the tension easing from Jess's body as she relaxed back into the soft, squishy leather, and was glad he was able to offer her a safe haven in his home.

It was strange to find his protective instincts on full alert where this woman was concerned.

Not that his other instincts were slouching far behind!

In fact, if he moved just slightly—as if unconsciously stretching out his legs—it would bring their hips together, then, if he turned towards her to say something, their thighs would press together, his arm could stretch along the back of the couch and—

The comedy show finished, and Jess stood up, taking his plate and clearing away the debris of their meal. He heard water running in the kitchen, but didn't follow her, realising it was more important to get his body back under control than to dry the dishes for her.

Dish-drying brought on a whole new range of problems. He'd already figured that out!

She came back into the living room but avoided the couch, going instead to his bookcase and kneeling to read the titles.

'*Davidson's Principles and Practice of Medicine*, not what you had in mind for bedtime reading?' he teased, as she shook her head at the work-oriented selection.

She threw a smile in his direction, then ran her fingers over the pile of heavy albums lying flat on the bottom shelf.

'Photos?'

'Family happy snaps!' he said lightly. He was always slightly embarrassed by the multitude of snapshots he'd hoarded over the years. 'I was given a camera when I was six and all I can say is it's a good thing my photography improved with age. My mother was fairly ruthless in discarding early accidents but there are still some headless classics among them.'

'May I look?' she asked.

'You've got to be joking! There's nothing more boring than other people's families!'

He saw the smile disappear and remembered her words

to Sarah about there only being her mother and herself. Had she hankered after a family?

'Would you really like to see them? I could give you the abridged show—perhaps the first and last.'

The smile almost returned.

'I'd really like to see them,' Jess told him, not adding that the urge to see him as a child was almost overwhelming.

He crossed the room and knelt beside her, then selected three of the fat binders.

'Come and sit on the couch. It's more comfortable and you'll be here for a while,' he said, and she went, reluctantly excited, excitedly reluctant.

'Is this you?' she asked, pointing to a child standing proudly on the steps of a large weatherboard house.

He leaned closer to look at the photo, and she could feel the outline of the muscles in his arm, see his chest move as he breathed, smell hospital and man and the faint remnants of a woodsy aftershave she'd first detected in the air in the bathroom.

'No, that's my friend Jeff. I'm behind the camera. I doubt there's one of me here at all.'

He flicked over a few pages, then found a family shot someone else must have taken.

'There I am,' he said, sounding slightly embarrassed although the blond child he pointed to looked handsome enough!

'You were white-blond back then?'

'A changeling, people said, but as you can see my hair darkened. In my late teens it turned this anaemic mouse brown.'

Jess moved so she could see the hair in question.

'I'd call it honey brown, sun-shot honey at the moment with all those golden streaks in it.'

He turned and their lips were so close she held her breath and waited for the kiss. But words came instead.

'That's a very pretty compliment,' he murmured. 'Now, are we making out here or looking at photos?'

He was giving her a choice—asking for her invitation.

She studied the lips, raised her gaze to the eyes, and saw the question repeated there.

'Making out? That's a very American expression! I think the photos, don't you?'

'Coward!'

'For the moment,' she said, then, wanting him to understand, added, 'It's too soon, Andrew, and too sudden, and just so overwhelming. Then there's all this other business tied up in it. How can I know what's real and what's reaction?'

Her eyes asked the questions now, begging him to understand.

He ran his hand lightly across her hair, disturbing it enough to let it escape from the confining ribbon. Then he plunged his fingers into its thickness and massaged her scalp, drawing her closer until he could drop a hint of a kiss on her lips.

'I can wait,' he said huskily, then he turned the page to show more photographs.

More shaken than she cared to admit, Jess forced herself to focus on the unfamiliar faces.

'Who are the girls?' she asked as the three appeared again and again.

'My sisters.'

He said it with pride, and as he gave names to the faces he betrayed his love, pleasing Jess that he was a man not afraid to admit to his feelings.

All his feelings?

'But they're all so dark,' she said, deciding the photos were a safer topic than emotions. 'Not one of them has that white-blond hair you had.'

He flipped another page to where one of the girls— Louise, she thought—was a teenager. Dressed for a dance or school formal, she wore a red satin ball gown and looked spectacular, with a swathe of dark hair falling straight and shiny to below her shoulder blades.

'They took after my father. He must have had strong genes because all three of them had his blue eyes and dark hair. I'm a throwback to my mother's father in looks, and my mother, who refused to accept mouse-brown and stayed blonde with the help of a good hairdresser, swears she was naturally as blonde as I was when she was young.'

'Have you photos of them—your parents?' Jess asked, then waited as he skipped over pages, fascinated by the movement of his fingers, seeing their suppleness, the tanned skin and strong white nails.

Imagined them raking across her back, teasing at her spine, touching her—

'Here they are.'

Andrew's voice jolted her out of thoughts so erotic she could feel that wretched heat showing up again in her cheeks.

'He's very handsome,' she managed. 'And she's lovely. What a great couple.'

She studied the pair, as she often studied couples in photographs or real life, wondering about the special chemistry required for people to stay together when so many partnerships fell apart.

'They look as if they like each other,' she said, and ran her fingers across the plastic cover protecting the image.

'Oh, they do!' Andrew assured her. 'Something we children never realised. I mean, as you grow up, you don't think of your parents as lovers but, boy, once the family all moved out those two were so pleased to be on their own again it was practically indecent.'

'I think that's great,' Jess told him, wondering if her mother had missed having someone, apart from a daughter, to love.

Wondering again about who had loved her mother.

And subsequently fathered herself?

Andrew was talking again, and she pushed away the unanswerable questions to concentrate on his words—and the pictures.

He'd opened the second book—older children.

'Not that they were always happy, my parents. In real life, I doubt anyone is. They argued from time to time— and as a kid I'd sometimes know things weren't quite right between them—but they must have worked through it because they certainly made it stick.'

'Here's me, growing up,' he added, pointing to a handsome lad of about seventeen. 'That's Shelley Ryan, my first true love.'

'She's very pretty,' Jess said, hiding the unexpected pang which either his words or the girl's attractive young image had caused.

'But not beautiful,' he said softly, and she turned to face him, felt her body heat, then melt and sway towards him. Her lips met his halfway, responding fervently, clinging to the kiss as if it might ease the dreadful aching need deep down inside her body.

Her response fired Andrew's body, but somewhere in the meld of novelty and desire a small voice issued warnings.

Go steady with this woman, she's different.

Alone.

Vulnerable.

And remember it's been a long time for you—don't mix lust with love. Don't cheat her with second best.

He filed the messages away, knowing they'd act as a brake when required, then gave himself up to the pleasure of kissing her.

The phone acted as an even more effective brake, right about the time his fingers found the buttons on the front of her uniform.

He reached over for it, but kept her clamped against his

side, fearing she'd bolt when she realised how far they'd almost gone.

He smoothed his hand across her hair, and rubbed his fingers against her neck, kneading at the muscles and tendons, silently telling her it was OK.

When he'd hung up he turned to her, saying calmly, 'Rowan's asked the neighbours but it seems your admirer is a spirit of some kind, floating by, invisible to all but those who believe.'

She shivered, and he cursed his attempt at humour.

'You're safe here, Jess,' he assured her, using the short version of her name for the first time. 'In every way. Safe with me, I promise you that.'

She looked into his eyes, her own so wide, so blue that he could easily have drowned in them.

'I guess I know that,' she admitted, then the well-kissed lips trembled into a smile. 'But the phone call was a blessing, wasn't it? I don't think we should go too far, too fast!'

He stifled the urge to leap off the couch, punch the air and yell, 'Yes!'

But the stifling took some doing.

As did speaking.

'A blessing,' he finally agreed with fitting solemnity, hiding his delight at the future implicit in her words.

'I think I'll go up to bed. It's been a long day, one way and another. May I take one of your photo albums? Look through the pictures?'

He was so affected by her request he forgot to kiss her goodnight, simply handing her one of the books, then watching her walk to the stairway.

'Goodnight,' she called softly back to him.

'Goodnight?' he muttered after her, as his body reminded him of just how long it had been celibate!

CHAPTER FIVE

HE COULD do this, Andrew decided late the following day when Jess had again been in Cas with him and had worked beside him while they'd stabilised a firewood contractor who'd slashed the calf of his leg with his chainsaw.

'Fancy having the courage to simply wrap the wound and drive to town for help,' Jessica remarked when they had a drip running into the patient's arm and morphine easing the pain. 'What now? Are you going to tackle the repairs or send him on?'

'We'll have a look and flush it as much as we can, assess the damage.'

He waited while she unwrapped the black singlet the man had used to cover the wound, and caught her shudder of reaction at the sight she revealed.

'The chain rips into everything it touches, so it's never a clean cut,' he explained. 'Add the fact that he moved when he felt it strike and complicated the wound with shallower abrasions—see, here and here. Then the chain itself wouldn't have been clean. Add the bits of debris it introduces and you get a very dirty wound.'

'So we leave it open to avoid infection? Can you afford to do that?'

Jess was flushing the ugly mess with warmed sterile water as she asked the question, while he put on a head-light for better illumination of the area and probed gently at the tissue.

'I think we'll have to send him on. There's nerve and blood vessel involvement, and some of these fragments look like bone, although the cut doesn't seem deep enough to have struck his fibula. His axillary vein's involved but he seems to have missed the arteries.'

'What do we do for him now?'

He was pleased at her swift response, and found he enjoyed working with her as a nurse—enjoyed her competency as much as having her near him.

'The bleeding's stopped, so how about if you call an ambulance, warn them it's a trip to town and tell them I want an attendant along to keep an eye on the patient. I'll wrap the wound in a sterile dressing to stop any outside infection and probably pray I've done the right thing.'

Jessica shot him a quizzical look but went to call the ambulance. It wasn't until later in the day, as they were driving home, that she asked about the prayer.

'Do you do that often—pray you've done the right thing?'

He glanced at her, surprised she'd picked up on such a throwaway comment, and saw from the intent look on her face it wasn't just an idle question.

'Often,' he admitted, then he sighed. 'Well, perhaps it's more hope than prayer. It's to do with the parameters of the job in country practice, Jess. Confines, some would say. I love surgery, especially delicate microscopic stuff, like joining tiny blood vessels and thread fine nerves.'

'But you need special equipment for microsurgery,' she protested. 'You'd have to be in a large regional centre at the very least to practise it.'

He shrugged and, wanting to talk but not yet ready to go home—fearing that whatever lay in wait there might break the feeling of contentment between them—he pulled the car into the car park that stood above a riverside picnic area. The grassy slope fell away to where willows and river gums held the river to its course. Glimpses of the green-brown water could be seen between the branches.

'I guess a lot of life is about compromise. We have enough equipment for me to have tackled those repairs today, but I had to weigh up the urgency of the need for surgery against the problems involved in doing it here. I'd have been in Theatre for up to four hours, taken Sarah from her patients to act as anaesthetist and needed a couple of nurses off the ward to assist.'

'But if it had been something urgent—something that couldn't wait?'

Her presence, so close within the metal cell of the car, was tangible, her interest adding to her appeal.

'Like a burr hole in the skull to release pressure from a haemorrhage? Or sewing on a severed digit?'

'Exactly.'

'If it's an extreme emergency, of course, we get all hands on deck and operate here, rather than risk the patient dying on the trip to town. We'd also do it for less exciting things like a burst appendix, because the longer the patient isn't treated the more chance there is of peritonitis taking hold.'

She nodded then smiled at him.

'All of which isn't diverting me from what I asked. OK, you're a country boy at heart, but Australia has any number of large regional cities far enough into the bush to count as country. Couldn't you practise the surgery you apparently enjoy in one of them and still have the delights of country life?'

He chuckled.

'Do I detect a note of sarcasm in your voice, Nurse Chapman, when you talk of the delights of country life?'

'No way! I haven't been here long, but already I appreciate the sense of—I can't explain it without making it sound like a put-down, but it's as if life moves at a slower pace. Yet things get done just the same.'

'More relaxed, less frenetic?'

She nodded in response.

'It gives people time to look around, see the beauty of the trees down by the river, the stripes of yellow and rust-red beneath their bark, the way the leaves droop towards the water, reaching down to kiss their shadows.'

'Reaching down to kiss their shadows!' he repeated softly, brushing his knuckles across her cheeks, aching to feel her lips on his, to taste her, touch her, take her as his woman.

'Shall we go home?' he asked, and the smile she gave him this time was far from certain, but it strengthened as he watched, then twinkled cheekily in her eyes.

'I guess we should, but to eat and sleep—not to do what you're thinking,' she told him. The lovely eyes asked for understanding, although the lips tormented him with other emotions. 'I don't want there to be regrets later. To get into something too quickly, then not be able to get out.'

He held up his hands.

'Not too far, too fast. I remember,' he said, then he brushed his fingers against her hair as he lowered his arms. 'But that's not going to stop me kissing you the very moment we're out of the public eye, so be warned, Miss Chapman, and pucker those lovely lips.'

Jess felt a thrill of anticipation, although the teasing laughter in his voice, the easy affection she could hear and feel between them, was almost as exciting as the promise of the kiss.

But not as electrifying as the real thing, she realised when they'd entered the house without a silent message of roses and moved into each other's arms to fulfil the promise.

'OK,' Andrew said, much later when they were in the kitchen, preparing their evening meal. 'The kisses are very nice. I like them. I'm all for kisses. But it's playing hell with my libido so just beware, Miss Jessica. I could inadvertently jump you any moment and it will be up to you to remind me of the ''go slow'' policy.'

'Why don't you go and have a shower?' she suggested. 'Cool down a little while I fix the dinner.'

He grumbled, grabbed her from behind and lifted her hair so he could press a kiss against the back of her neck.

Reaction jolted through her so strongly she knew he'd felt it.

'Cold shower for one, or warm one for two?' he said temptingly, and she had to break away before she weakened and plunged into an affair with him and be damned to the consequences.

What was holding her back? she wondered when he'd finally departed, leaving her feeling very alone in the kitchen.

Time was one issue. They'd only met a week ago on Monday and today was Thursday—eleven days couldn't be considered a reasonable getting-to-know-you period.

But her friends often plunged into affairs after a single meeting.

'You're not your friends!' The echo of her mother's voice provided resonance to the words and she knew exactly why she was trying to slow this roller-coaster down. Why she'd always been cautious—overly so at times.

Until Robert, when she'd rushed in to escape her grief and loss—and been so badly burned.

'That dinner ready yet?'

Andrew's reappearance—his gleaming skin, damp-darkened hair, casually clad body—banished all thoughts of Robert, and the gloom his memory always evoked.

'Not quite,' she admitted, realising she hadn't done a thing since he'd departed.

'Then leave it to me,' he announced, taking her in his arms again and kissing her soundly. 'Go take a shower yourself. It will wake you up as you've obviously been sleeping on the job.'

The kiss deepened, his tongue parting her lips, teasing her to kiss him back, tempting her to forget restraint.

'I'll have that shower,' she muttered, grabbing the last vestiges of willpower before they were annihilated by his potent appeal. She pushed herself away, and was again surprised by the emotion she caught in the darkened green of his eyes.

She showered, then came downstairs, bringing with her the photo album she'd borrowed the previous evening.

'Had enough of Andrew as a lad?' he asked, and she smiled at him, grateful for his understanding—for keeping his distance. The restraints were back in place, although definitely weakened by the passion they'd shared in a couple of simple kisses.

'I thought I'd like to see the others,' she told him. 'Not now, of course, but maybe later.'

She imagined he'd guessed why but said it anyway.

'As an only child of a single parent, I suppose there's a deep-seated psychological reason for me liking family albums.'

She reached the dining-room table and he pulled out the chair and held it as she slipped into it. Then he rested his hand on her shoulder.

'I don't think it makes you either kinky or peculiar! I love looking at images of other people's lives myself, and I had all the family I wanted.'

He'd served the meal, lamb chops with fresh vegetables, in the kitchen and put her plate in front of her, his own opposite, then sat down.

'But you can't have been that isolated from relatives. Must have had some family somewhere, unless your mother was also found under a cabbage.'

He wasn't looking at her, concentrating on separating meat from the chop bone.

'Cousins, aunts, grandparents on either side,' he continued. 'No one has no family.'

She did a little surgery of her own while she wondered how to answer. Whether to tell him.

Decided not to, as she was still so uncertain—not so much of him but of where her quest would lead.

'No one,' she said firmly. 'My mother was an only child, pushed from the nest when I was on the way. I don't know who my father was. The only thing I ever knew about him was that my mother had loved him very much, but that it was not to be.'

Jessica's words made Andrew feel a coldness which was hard to shake. It wasn't that she'd sounded bitter. In fact, bitter might have been preferable. It was the total lack of emotion in her voice that rattled him—a lack so at odds with the passion of her kisses that it didn't seem possible such diversity could exist within one body.

'One of the albums has photos of my parents when they were young, if you're really into families. And another has a string of weddings in them. My sisters had a thing going with weddings for a couple of years—all of them lining up at one time or another. Although only once—so far—one each, I mean.'

She smiled politely as he made a nonsense of the sentence, and nodded to show she understood.

'The chops are lovely,' she said, apparently deciding to do her own change of conversational topic. 'That's one thing I've noticed out here in the country. Good meat.'

'And good company with whom to eat it?' he teased, wanting the smile to warm a little, although her warmer smiles did so much damage to his innards he was likely to get a hernia before long.

The smile did warm, then became the genuine article—not the full-blown, thousand-watt effort but good enough.

'I forgot to tell you. I phoned Tamworth about your man with the cut leg before I went off duty,' she said. 'He'd just come out of Theatre and was in Recovery. They've sewed him up and the white flecks you found *were* bone—apparently he'd killed a beast and had been using his chainsaw to cut it up. It was animal bone.'

'I should have guessed there was something fishy about it all. Most of the firewood carters work on private properties, cutting up old fallen trees. I wondered why he hadn't simply gone to the homestead and phoned for help, rather than driving himself into town. He'd stolen an animal and killed it for meat. The carcass will be out there somewhere.'

'Will you report it?' Jess asked, then watched him shrug.

'The way I look at it, he must have been hungry to do it. And if he'd done it before, my guess is that the farmer, missing a beast, wouldn't have let him back on the place again, so perhaps we'll let it go as a one-off and hope his injury has taught him a lesson.'

'You're a kind man, Andrew Kendall,' Jess said, her pleasure in his kindness out of all proportion to the act. 'Now, you cooked so I'll do the dishes.'

She had to stand up before she could reach across the table and take his hand, and hold it as she told him how she felt about his kindness.

The dishes finished, they sat together on the lounge, comfortable in each other's company, touching, sometimes kissing, but without the heat of their earlier exchanges.

Waiting, but seemingly content to wait, Jess decided.

'Tomorrow's Friday and we go to work, then there's a weekend—we'll both be off duty, although I've Outpatients Saturday morning and then I'm on call.' Andrew held her right hand and teased at the palm with his thumb as he gravely outlined what she already knew.

'So?' Jess asked, tempting fate because she guessed what he was thinking.

'So we'll have known each other twelve days by then,' he said. 'Lived together for five of them without a cross word being spoken. And we'll have two whole days—minus time out for mishaps and emergencies—to spend together. Anything you'd particularly like to do?'

Excitement flared like rocket fuel inside her and the warnings of her head lost strength.

'Did you have something special in mind?' she teased.

He turned and took her in his arms and the contentment

vanished as an all-consuming hunger fired her blood and made her weak with wanting him.

'Jess, my Jess, my Jessica!'

The murmured words were like a prayer, the touch of his lips an offering of such sweet delight she shivered under the onslaught. She felt his fingers fumble at the buttons on her shirt but was too busy undoing his to worry, or to stop the hands impatiently pushing aside the fine cotton and reaching for her tautly heavy breasts.

'The phone will ring, there's nothing surer,' he muttered, as she kissed his neck while he nuzzled at her ear. 'And I'm rushing you again, I know I am.'

She eased herself away until she could look into his face.

'Do you want to go on? Risk me freaking out again and asking you to stop?'

'Or the bloody phone ringing? Of course I want to go on, sweet woman. On and on for ever, but I'll be content with what you give.'

She kissed him then, so overwhelmed by the promise implicit in those words that she knew she wouldn't call a halt, but would join him in the fulfilment of both their desires and be happy to take whatever consequences might ensue.

He returned the kiss, with humility as well as passion, and she felt gentleness as well as strength, a modicum of love perhaps, as well as physical attraction.

And now that she'd virtually invited him, the pace slowed, the kisses suddenly so sweet she sipped them as she might nectar, while he seemed to savour her, all of her, through her lips and skin.

'Damn!'

'What?'

She was plunged so quickly from bliss to brightness that it took her a moment to work out he must have turned off the light some time ago and had just switched it back on to find the phone.

'I knew this would happen!' he grumbled. 'But next weekend—not this one but the next—Sarah will be on duty and the phone will be unplugged for the entire two days.'

He lifted the receiver and barked, 'Yes?' His hand found hers and held it tightly.

He mumbled something else then dropped the receiver and turned to smooth her hair back from her face.

'You'll probably be on duty next weekend. I'm doomed to celibacy—to living with the world's most beautiful woman and never getting to bed with her.'

'Hospital?' she asked, and watched him nod.

'I've a patient in labour. I've got to go.'

He stood up and was about to move away when he turned back to look at her. 'I don't want to leave you here alone,' he muttered, and raked his fingers through his hair. 'Damn the woman! Why tonight?'

Jess stood up and touched him on the arm.

'Why any night?' she said gently. 'It had to happen some time—leaving me alone. And it will happen again. You can't put me under your personal twenty-four-hour protection.'

His grin was rueful, but his eyes were worried, and suddenly she didn't want him worried.

'I'll come with you,' she suggested.

His forehead rumpled as he considered this then he touched her lightly on the chin.

'You know, that's not a bad idea. Go get your night gear, toothbrush and clothes for tomorrow. If this proves an all-nighter, I can snatch some sleep during the day. You're on duty in the morning and need to get some rest. I'll park you with Sarah in the flat.'

Andrew saw her wince at his choice of words, but she didn't argue, although her body language as she walked with him to the car a few minutes later told him he'd hurt her.

'You're not a nuisance to me so don't go thinking it,'

he growled, when they were on their way through night-quiet streets.

'Of course I'm a nuisance to you,' she snapped right back at him. 'If I weren't here you wouldn't have to worry what to do with me. You wouldn't have nutters leaving roses on your doorstep, or have the police questioning your neighbours. I should go back to the cabin. After all, roses won't hurt me. Some women would be flattered.'

Her voice wavered slightly on the last remark and it was all he could do not to haul her into his arms and kiss her again—kiss her until she forgot everything but him, and the attraction that had somehow flared between them.

He was telling himself it was impossible to accomplish this while he was driving when she charged into battle again.

'And now you're dumping me on Sarah! I'm sure she'll like that. Particularly if it means the nutter will target her next.'

'Hey, don't go to pieces on me now!' he said, realising there could be hysteria behind her anger. 'You can't let whoever's doing this to you see they've got you rattled.'

'I am not going to pieces.' Jessica stood on the hysteria idea by speaking firmly and deliberately—if with some venom. 'And no one—apart from you—is going to see me rattled!'

'Good for you!' he told her, driving into the hospital grounds and again parking close to the flat. 'At least Sarah's still up. Let's tell her she's got visitors.'

But as he switched off the engine and silence fell between them he turned to her and repeated his praise.

'You're special, Jess.' He said the words more softly, then leaned across and kissed her on the lips. 'I like a woman with spunk.'

Her lips met his, hesitated, then clung, returning the salute with a fervour that reefed the air from his lungs in a great whoosh of breath and made his body stir in a most inappropriate fashion for someone on his way to work.

'I've got to go, but hold that thought,' he murmured, seemingly aeons later, shoving his fingers into her glorious hair and trapping her so he could examine the wondrous beauty of her face.

He brushed a final kiss across her lips then forced himself out of the car, coming around to open the passenger door and help her out.

'You could try a smile,' he suggested gently, although the expression of wonder on her face made him want to leap for joy, and dance and sing. 'The dazed look might be misinterpreted.'

She tried a smile, so hesitant it made him want to kiss her again, but at that moment Sarah, no doubt alerted by car doors opening outside her living-room window, appeared at the door.

'How nice. Midnight visitors!' she said. 'Are you coming in?'

'Jess is,' Andrew replied, steering his precious new love towards the light. 'Can you put her up? I've a baby on the way so might not make it home and I don't want to leave her on her own, her being new in town and all that.'

He felt Jessica's shoulders shake as she chuckled at his weak excuse. It was good he could make her laugh. Laughing together was important.

'Well, off you go!' Sarah interrupted his musings and waved him towards the hospital. 'I'll take care of Jess.'

Was everyone calling her Jess?

Better than Kristie.

He frowned as he headed for the maternity suites. The name rang a vague bell, but maybe that was because he, like everyone else who knew about the note, was trying to force a connection.

'Kristie, Kristie, Kristie!'

He hadn't realised he was muttering it aloud until his

patient, Sue Redman, said, 'Did I tell you that's what I'm going to call this baby if it's a girl?'

He snapped his mind to attention and focussed it on his patient.

'Why?'

'After Caroline Cordell,' Sue replied, while he listened to Jill Ross, the midwife on duty, fill him in on the timing of pains and the dilatation of Sue's cervix.

'Cam's daughter? The one who died?' Andrew asked, sorry now he hadn't listened more closely to that particular piece of gossip. 'Car accident, wasn't it?'

'Of course, you wouldn't have heard,' Sue said, and promptly launched, between pains, into the saga of Caroline Cordell's death and a well known TV producer's drug addiction.

How someone in a country town could have known so many intimate details of a stranger's life was a mystery to Andrew, but telling the story was distracting Sue from her pain so he listened, then remembered where the talk had begun.

'But what's the connection between Caroline Cordell's death and the name Kristie?' he asked.

Sue gave a long-suffering sigh that said, as plainly as words would have, that he didn't know *anything*.

'Kristie was the part she played in *18 Park Lane*, the TV show,' she explained, and Andrew felt disappointment kick inside him. Unless Jessica was connected with a TV show, that was another dead end.

Sue was still talking, apparently about the show.

'So, of course, they had to change ever so many episodes which had been filmed ahead because it would have been tactless, I guess, having Kristie still alive on the show when Caroline was dead.'

'Totally tactless,' Andrew agreed in heartfelt tones. 'So what did they do? Kill Kristie off?'

'Well, no,' Sue answered slowly. 'Although, seeing that

Caroline *was* dead and couldn't come back to the part in a few years, like some of the soap stars do, you would have thought they would have killed her off. But I guess that wouldn't have been too nice either. They sent her back to the country, where she'd come from originally. I wonder if they wrote the part that way in the beginning because Caroline came from the country herself.'

Another contraction stopped the flow of words, but not for long, and when Sue's husband, Neil, arrived, having successfully disposed of the couple's older child with a grandmother, he turned out to be as great a fan of the show as his wife.

By the time Christopher Redman entered the world an hour later, Andrew felt he knew the flatmates at *18 Park Lane* intimately, although he was still confused about who was currently 'seeing' whom.

Intimately!

CHAPTER SIX

ALTHOUGH she felt safe and secure in the spare bedroom of Sarah's flat, Jess found sleep difficult to capture. The dynamics between herself and Andrew had shifted, and the checks and balances she'd hoped to put in place had been negated by the attraction between them.

So, what now? She'd more or less promised. More or less given in already—or would have if the baby hadn't decided to arrive.

But nothing should go on at work, she reminded herself, which gave her another day to consider the situation.

Having made that decision, she finally dozed, but woke to unfamiliar darkness when the first calls of the butcher birds heralded the dawn. Sliding out of bed as soon as daylight began to chase the shadows from the room, she headed quietly towards the bathroom where she dressed in the casual clothes she'd worn the previous evening. She'd walk down to the caravan park and clean out the cabin, perhaps check on the rose garden as she went past—see if any of the blooms looked familiar.

'And just where do you think you're going?' Sarah asked, appearing, bleary-eyed, in her doorway as Jess tip-toed past.

'I couldn't sleep,' she said, and explained about the cabin.

Sarah frowned and shook her head.

'Look,' she said, 'I know it's daylight and it sounds rational and you'd probably be perfectly safe, but I promised Andrew I'd watch over you and I have no intention of traipsing around outdoors at this hour of the morning. I don't do early mornings!'

'I'm sorry. I shouldn't have disturbed you,' Jess said, and Sarah smiled at her.

'You didn't. I was awake, and thinking about your problem. I was just reluctant to get out of bed, especially as I'm out of coffee and don't start well without it. If you want to do something really useful, how about you nip over to the kitchen and talk whoever's doing breakfast into giving you a few teaspoonfuls of instant in a cup?'

Jess wanted to argue, but knew she'd already put Sarah out with her late-night arrival. She nodded and was about to leave when Sarah added, 'Tell them it's a loan. I'll repay it when I've shopped.'

Jess chuckled and was still smiling at the thought of the doctor scurrying across with half a cup of coffee granules to replace the 'loan' when she entered the kitchen.

'You're up early.' Mrs Astbury, the cook, was herself on duty early. As Jess walked in she was piling bacon on a plate already decorated with a couple of long sausages and two fried eggs. 'I'm just feeding Joe here before he starts work. Doesn't eat enough to keep a sparrow alive, I reckon.'

Joe, whom Jess recognised as one of the gardeners, ducked his head at her in an embarrassed kind of way, then smiled. The smile transformed the expression on his face from that of a fairly ordinary-looking young man, possibly in his early twenties, into one of such sweet beauty that Jess smiled back at him.

'Looks good,' she said, nodding towards his plate.

'Mrs Astbury's the best,' he said, then turned his attention back to the food.

Jess explained her errand, and drew a chuckle from the cook when she said the loan would be repaid.

'Bless her heart,' Mrs Astbury said, spooning instant coffee liberally into a small jar. 'She can have as much coffee as she likes because she's been a joy to have around. Some of the locums we've had here wouldn't give the nurses the time of day, let alone lower themselves to talk to the domestic staff.'

Jess returned to the flat where she presented Sarah with both the coffee and the compliment.

'Joe was there, one of the gardeners. I should have asked him about the roses.'

Sarah seemed to consider that for a moment before she answered. 'I don't know. Didn't Rowan say he couldn't tell for certain that the first bloom came from here? And perhaps it's best to leave the police in charge of asking questions. If we start butting in, we'll all end up with bits and pieces of information, and no one will have enough to put it together.'

'I suppose you're right,' Jess agreed, but she hoped she'd bump into the lad with the lovely smile again later. He might let her have some roses to take to Mrs Cochrane, who often talked about the garden and especially admired the roses.

And thinking of Mrs Cochrane...

'Do you know what time they get going in the annexe? I could dress for work then pop up there, maybe help with the morning duties.'

'That's a kind thought. I'm sure enough of them are awake for whoever's on duty to appreciate a hand.'

Sarah fixed the coffee and waved her hand towards the cereal and bread she'd set out on the table.

'Toaster on the bench, milk and fruit in the refrigerator. Help yourself while I go back to bed to finish waking up. I like to stick to a routine which eases me gently into the day.'

Jess helped herself, cleaned up the kitchen, dressed and, with an hour to spare before she was due on duty, walked over to the annexe.

'An extra hand? You're a godsend,' the aide on duty greeted her. 'I'll finish the men but you might look in on Miss Finch in four and Mrs Allen in seven. They're both early risers. Just poke your head around the door and if either of them are stirring ask if they want to get up.'

Miss Finch was sitting on the edge of her bed.

'I've been contemplating walking across to the bathroom by myself, or ringing the bell for someone to help. I do so want a shower this morning, but Mrs Rogers is always so particular I don't shower without someone here. I hate ringing the bell—it's like summoning a maid. Not nice for the girls, who are always so good and helpful.'

Jess steadied her on the short walk to the *en suite* bathroom, supervised the desired ablutions, then helped the elderly woman dress for the day.

'I'm right now you've got me walking so I can wander out into the garden on my own,' Miss Finch told her. 'But you could check on Connie next door. I thought I heard her moving about earlier, and although she's used to having maids, having grown up that way, you know, she doesn't like to use the bell either.'

So, instead of checking on Mrs Allen in seven, Jess tapped quietly on the door of room five and pushed it open.

Mrs Cochrane was sitting up in bed.

'Come in, come in, don't hover,' she said testily. 'Open the curtains, could you? I'd like to see the day.'

Jess crossed the room and pulled the heavy drapes aside.

'Oh, it's you. Why are you here?' the old lady said, her voice much firmer this early in the morning than it was when Jess usually saw her in the late afternoon.

'I was at work early—I'm not due on duty until eight— so I thought I might be useful here.'

'Well, I'm all for girls making themselves useful,' Mrs Cochrane told her. 'Where did you say you were from?'

'Sydney,' Jess replied, although she couldn't recall Mrs Cochrane ever having shown the slightest interest in her as a person. 'Would you like the doors opened as well? It's a lovely morning.'

The old lady nodded, and Jess opened the doors that led
onto the wide verandah.

'The roses are beautiful,' she said, looking towards the
beds that flanked the back verandah of the hospital where
a gardener, possibly Joe, was digging weeds. 'Do you like
roses?'

Mrs Cochrane lifted her hand and held it towards Jess.

'Not when I'm still getting over a nasty infection from
a thorn,' she said.

Jess crossed to the bed and took hold of the delicate
hand, noticing the frail bones and ropy blue veins beneath
the almost translucent white skin. She battled the welter of
emotions churning inside her, recognising anger, despair
and sadness with, just possibly, a tiny pinch of love.

'It still looks puffy,' she said, finally focussing on the
dark scab of the scratch and the slightly swollen flesh
around it. 'Are you on antibiotics?'

'Again!' Mrs Cochrane told her. 'I took one lot, then had
to take another. I told young Dr McPhee a rose bush
shouldn't have that much power over a human being.'

Jess smiled at her indignation.

'What about spiders?' she teased gently. 'They're so
small we can squash them with ease, but some of them can
kill faster than you could get to a doctor.'

'My husband died of a spider bite,' Mrs Cochrane said,
and once again Jess was overwhelmed by too many feelings
to handle all at once.

'I—I didn't know,' she stuttered. 'I wouldn't have
brought it up. I'm so sorry.'

'Don't be.' The old lady patted Jess's arm with her free
hand. 'You weren't to guess and it was so long ago I can't
feel the ache of it any more. The pain of the loss. Not like
with Ginny. That pain never went away.'

Jess forced the air trapped in her lungs out through her
mouth, then breathed in a fresh supply, reminding herself
not to hold too tightly to the hand that lay in hers.

'Ginny?' she said, pleased her voice hadn't wavered too noticeably.

'My daughter. She went away.'

Mrs Cochrane withdrew her hand from Jess's and lay back against her pillows.

Jess glanced at her watch. It was five to eight—she had to go! But could she leave now when she was so close?

'She went away?' she repeated quietly, hoping to prompt more conversation—longing for it, yet dreading it at the same time.

Mrs Cochrane looked at her for a moment, then turned her head away.

'That's not true,' she whispered, and Jess saw the tears streaming down her soft, lined cheeks. 'I sent her away!'

The words were so soft they were barely audible, but the anguish that accompanied them filled the room and swamped Jess like a tidal wave.

She wanted to say something, to help the old woman through this moment of grief, but her own tears were flowing now and she couldn't bear to think someone might see them—might ask why.

With swift steps she crossed the room, leaving through the French doors, swiping at the moisture with her fingers because she'd forgotten to pack a handkerchief when she'd left Andrew's house the previous evening.

Heading blindly across the grass between the buildings, she prayed there was no one around, hoped for a few moments of peace to settle her nerves and get a grip on her emotions. There was a washroom on the back verandah. If she could make it that far, use a paper towel to mop up all these tears—

She ran slap bang into a solid chest and knew immediately it was Andrew.

'Hey, I came back hoping to see you before you started work, but didn't expect quite such a fervent greeting.'

He spoke lightly but his voice was tight with anger and

she knew he'd seen the tears because the arms around her
were more comforting than seductive.

'Trouble?'

She shook her head and, now that his shirt had absorbed
most of the wetness, eased herself out of his arms.

'Not enough sleep!' she mumbled. 'It left me a bit emotional.'

'Sure!' he said dryly, but he didn't push for further explanation, merely stood, strong and solid, in front of her.

'Your baby?' she asked, anxious to get things back on
an even footing again. 'Did it finally arrive? Did *you* get
any sleep?'

His lips smiled but his eyes were grave as he answered.

'A boy, and, yes, I had some sleep, but I'll head home
again when I've done my round and the outpatients session.
If I'm needed in Cas someone will phone me.'

He paused and she knew he was waiting for a better
explanation from her than lack of sleep, but some things
she couldn't explain.

'Well, I'd better get to work,' she said. 'See you later.'

'That you will,' he said gently, and Jess shivered as the
words sneaked under her skin and fired her blood.

Perhaps getting involved with him wasn't a good idea.

Too distracting, apart from anything else.

Although not getting involved wasn't really an option, she
realised later. It was after lunch and she knew Andrew had
cancelled his golf game to catch up on some surgery, but
what she hadn't expected was her own change in duties.

'Kelly, our regular scrub nurse, has gone home with a
migraine,' Helen explained. 'I know you've done theatre
work before. Would you mind?'

Mind? When it offered her the opportunity to see
Andrew at work in a different field?

Jess assured Helen she'd be happy to do it and headed

for the suite of rooms, meeting Sarah, already garbed in green scrubs, in the anteroom.

'I'm the anaesthetist,' Sarah explained. 'A simple tonsillectomy first up, then fun, fun, fun—haemorrhoids! Are you here to scrub?'

'I'm circulating. Katie's been promoted to scrub,' Jess told her, as she stripped off her uniform and pulled on the first pair of loose theatre trousers that came to hand.

'Andrew's, I'd say,' Sarah said, smiling as Jess whipped the huge garment off and riffled through the pile for something that looked smaller.

'They seem to come in large or larger,' she complained.

Sarah nodded. 'Happens all the time in country hospitals. I now bring my own supply and get the hospital to launder them.'

She pointed to her name inked across the front of her shirt, then turned to show a similar identifying brand across the seat of her pants.

'Gets a laugh if nothing else.'

Jess was busy rolling up the legs of the trousers she'd settled on when the door opened and Andrew's arrival made the room seem very small.

'Very cute,' he said, smiling at the ballooning pants, then letting his gaze rise to take in her upper body, naked except for a neat white cotton bra.

She felt the heat begin and grabbed a shirt, dragging it ruthlessly over her head as Sarah excused herself and left the room.

'You scrubbing?' he asked, repeating Sarah's question, but his eyes were saying other things, so distracting it was all she could do to shake her head in a negative response to the question.

'I'm further down the pecking order,' she managed to explain, although the eyes still tormented her.

She slid her feet out of her shoes and took the next step

towards the sterile barrier, slipping on paper slippers before entering the scrub room.

Andrew's clogs were in the doorway, with 'A.K.' printed across the toes.

A.K.—a man she'd only heard of until last week, yet whom she now felt she knew so well.

A few minutes later they were all in place—gowned, scrubbed, gloved and masked. The child, having been se-dated with his mother still by his side, prior to entering the Theatre, lay like an insubstantial shadow beneath the sheet.

As circulating nurse, all Jess had to do was hover by the spare tray of sterilised instruments—a gofer if anything was needed, an extra hand to be called upon in an emergency. It gave her time to watch Andrew at the work he loved, to admire his swift, sure-hand movements.

And brood over how close Katie, an attractive redhead Jess knew was between boyfriends, stood to him.

Andrew talked as he worked, which didn't surprise Jess. He talked his way through most things! After a few minutes, the novelty of hearing him detail each step wore off, and she realised his voice had a calming effect in the Theatre.

'Tube!' he'd said as Sarah had nodded for him to begin, but he had already taken the nasopharyngeal tube from Katie and was inserting it.

'Packing for the throat.'

Katie did that while he fixed a clamp to keep the small mouth open and hold the tongue out of the way.

'Toothed forceps.' Katie passed him the instrument and Jess watched him take the tiny knob of left tonsil and pull it gently forward.

'Scalpel.'

It was slapped into his hand and again he talked through his method, explaining how he was cutting through the mu-cous membrane then gradually stripping the tiny pad of glandular tissue from its roots. He cauterised the bleeding vessels while Katie used suction to clear the child's mouth, then he began on the other side, repeating the procedure and talking all the time.

When the operation had finished and the anaesthetic reversed, Sarah took the child through to the recovery room and spoke to the nurse on duty there, while Jess helped Katie and Andrew strip off their soiled gloves, gowns and masks, scrub again, then don clean sterile gear.

She said little, enjoying being back in Theatre without the fears her relationship with Robert had generated.

'You didn't take long to snaffle him,' Katie said, nodding towards Andrew who'd crossed the brightly lit room and was speaking quietly to Sarah.

Jess shrugged. It would be all around the hospital that she was living in his house. She had to keep it light.

'He's not exactly snaffled,' she said. 'He was with me when I ran into trouble. Taking me home was his good deed for the day.'

'And keeping you there his reward?' Katie teased.

It was good-natured banter, but it bothered Jess, making her wonder if her presence in Andrew's house could cause gossip that might harm him.

The question pricked at her conscience as she waited through the next operation, and lingered as she walked up to the annexe to spend some more time with Mrs Cochrane, knowing Andrew wouldn't be ready to leave for another hour.

Although this morning's visit had shaken her, Jess knew she had to pursue that tiny crack in the older woman's defences.

She set thoughts of Andrew aside as she nodded to Bob and promised to join him in a board game the following day, then went along the corridor to tap on Mrs Cochrane's door.

'Would you like me to read to you this afternoon?' she asked.

The frail old lady was sitting by the door, her figure dwarfed by the high back of an old armchair.

'Perhaps you could sit a while,' she answered. 'You're very restful company.'

Jess fancied she could hear sadness in the quavery voice and see new lines in the finely wrinkled skin.

Was she unwell, or had this morning's admission upset her?

Would bringing up the subject again make things better or worse?

Jess pushed aside the unexpected pity she felt, and brought it up anyway.

'Do you want to talk about your daughter? About Ginny?'

Faded blue eyes tracked towards her, studied her for a moment.

'I never have. Not to anyone!' Mrs Cochrane whispered.

Jess held her breath, knowing so much lay in the balance—in one fractious woman's decision to talk or not to talk.

'She was pregnant.' The words were practically inaudible but they played like icy fingers up and down Jess's spine. 'He was married. So shameful—that was all I thought. All I considered. Myself, my shame. Not Ginny, or her hurt, her problem. Or the child.'

She lifted her wounded hand and touched Jess on the cheek.

'I was selfish. Pig-headed. Wrong.'

She closed her eyes and Jess saw the thin chest rise and fall with rhythmic precision. Mrs Cochrane had said her piece then drifted off to sleep.

Exhausted by emotion?

Or by the burden of regret she'd carried for so long?

Jess tiptoed away, knowing she was one step closer, understanding more.

A married man!

And she'd come close to repeating history with Robert.

Had her mother known her lover was married?

Had it been a love so strong she'd felt it didn't matter?

Until last week, Jess would have found that hard to believe. No love could have been so strong.

But now?

Since she'd met Andrew?

Would him being married have stopped the chemistry between them?

She made her way to Sarah's flat where she retrieved her hastily bundled belongings, then walked around the hospital building. She'd wait for Andrew by the car.

When she reached the rose garden she paused and, for the first time since the original bud had been delivered, drank in the subtle perfume and admired the display.

She bent to smell a cluster of full-blown pink blooms, and once again felt icy fingers tap-dance on her spine. Different fingers. Someone watching.

Pretending nonchalance, she straightened and looked around. There were up to a dozen people within view and she told herself she was being stupid. That was Helen on the verandah with one of the hospital board members who often popped in, and Mrs Astbury talking to someone outside the kitchen.

A blue uniform told her a nurse was walking a patient along the verandah and a pink uniform, moving swiftly, suggested an aide was on a mission of some kind. Another patient in a chair, and two elderly women walking slowly across the grass back towards the annexe. Probably the women who tended the gardens with such love and devotion.

No strangers. No one out of place.

She walked down to the car and leaned her back against it, watching the scene, her eyes alert for a watcher.

However, the first new figure to come into view was

Andrew, and she felt the tension ease from her body and the thrill of anticipation take its place.

'Are you OK?' he asked, his expression grave.

She wondered if he'd sensed her fear then remembered he'd seen her tears earlier in the day. The thrill of anticipation was dampened by those memories, but she assured him she was fine and climbed into the car.

He touched her lightly on the knee and smiled, then started the engine.

'Want to talk about it?' he prompted as they drove away.

She shook her head, although she knew that holding back would hurt him.

'Not yet,' she told him, implying that she would at some time in the future.

He didn't push it, simply driving home, asking how she felt about Chinese—the food, not the people—and asserting it was time they ate out for a change. After all, it was Friday night—end of the week.

'You don't have to court me, you know,' she said, smiling at his enthusiasm when she agreed to go out.

'I don't want to court you,' he told her. 'I want to flaunt you, to show off my woman to the world—well, Riverview at least.'

'I'm not your woman yet,' she reminded him, although his possessive words had sent tremors of delight zapping through her body.

'Oh, yes, you are,' he said firmly.

The reached the house and Andrew parked the car in the carport, explaining that Sarah was on call for the night and they could walk downtown to the restaurant.

He got out first—a habit he'd developed so he could check the doorstep for unwanted offerings of flowers. It was bare and he was tempted to hope the harassment had ceased.

Tempted also to hope that his love would eventually confide in him. So many things had happened to confirm his earlier impression that Jess had a sadness within her that went beyond her mother's death and a doomed love affair.

The tears this morning were another glimpse of something not quite right.

'So, do you want first shower or is tonight the night we save water and shower together?' he asked, turning back to where she'd paused by some bright blue flowers and was gazing at them with the kind of wonderment he'd prefer she reserved for him.

She glanced up and smiled.

'You go first. I'd like to cut a little bunch of these forget-me-nots.' She hesitated, then added tentatively, 'If that's all right with you?'

His heart did an extra beat that she could even ask.

'Of course it's all right with me, you foolish woman. Cut the lot if you like, whatever you want, whenever you want it, Jess. That's what I'd like to offer you.'

He saw her smile falter and the quick blinking of her eyelids and knew he'd made her cry.

'Happy tears this time, I hope?' he said gently, joining her in the garden and putting his arm around her shoulders.

'Happy tears,' she confirmed, and she leaned on him for a minute so that he felt a sense of such peace and contentment he feared to move lest he lost it.

'Go and have your shower,' she finally told him, nudging him away with her hip.

He moved, but not immediately, kissing her cheek before leaving her side. It had so many facets, this love he felt for her. The depth of it—the fondness and delight as well as the sexual attraction. It was like a polished stone that gave off different colours in the sunlight.

He walked inside, chuckling at such daft romantic fancies.

Jess followed him to the kitchen, found some scissors and went back out to pick the flowers. She made a loose bunch of them and, after searching unsuccessfully for a vase in Andrew's kitchen, set them in a little glass of water and carried them through to the coffee-table in the living room.

One of the photo albums was lying there, and she flicked it open, seeing his parents' wedding photos, looking at the faces of the young couple, wondering if the older version would like her. Approve of her for their son.

Which brought back fears that they were moving too far too fast, but she shrugged them off, knowing the commitment had already been made.

CHAPTER SEVEN

ANDREW came downstairs in a dark green shirt Jess hadn't seen before, his hair combed neatly back from his forehead although she knew it wouldn't last that way once it was dry.

Dry! The word described her mouth as she looked at him and thought about what would happen later—what she wanted so badly it made her shake to consider it.

'I won't be long,' she managed to mutter, and she fled past him, up the steps, knowing that if he touched her, or she touched him, Chinese food would be forgotten in the all-consuming fire they were both fighting to control.

She dressed in a long, finely woven cotton shift—the blue of the forget-me-nots she'd plucked from his garden earlier. Brushed her hair until it hung like a shining mantle on her shoulders. Touched her lips with a muted pink lipstick, and stroked a glittering silver blue pencil close to her eyelashes. Not too much, but enough to add some colour to her pale and wondering face.

She walked back downstairs, her knees shaking, and found him smiling at her from the lounge they'd shared each evening.

'OK, let's eat!' he said, standing up and moving to take her hand.

She guessed the words had been intended to set her at ease, but the look in his eyes told her he was as nervous as she was—as filled with an anticipation that mixed delight and apprehension in equal measure.

'The Red Dragon—really original name that—Chinese restaurant in this town is superb. Comes of having a real

Chinese family running it, I guess.' He took her hand and led her out the door, pausing to lock it behind him.

She guessed he was talking to cover how he felt and let him ramble on, telling her the names of neighbours as they strolled past houses she usually saw from the car.

'Should we be walking hand in hand?' she asked, when someone had called to Andrew from their front porch. 'Isn't it like making a public announcement in a town this size?'

His fingers tightened as if he feared she'd pull away.

'That's why I'm doing it,' he told her. 'Best to broadcast it before the gossips start in on us. At least this way it can be talked about quite openly.'

Jess wasn't certain how she should feel about this theory, but as she knew so few people in the town she accepted his judgement and walked on. Besides, her hand felt cosy tucked into Andrew's. Secure, and comfortable, and safe!

The cooking smells began their work on her taste buds as they reached the restaurant and pushed through the glass beads strung across the open door, and suddenly she was ravenously hungry.

Andrew introduced her to Mrs Lo, a plump woman of indeterminate age.

'Mrs Lo has been here for as long as most people in the town can remember,' Andrew told her, and the woman beamed at him as if he'd paid her the ultimate compliment.

'Real Australian now,' she told Jess proudly, although the 'r's in the first two words still gave the older woman trouble. 'You sit, both of you. I'll get something special to begin.'

'Don't you order?' Jess asked, as the hostess disappeared.

'Never,' Andrew said. 'She'll bring out prawn toasts and some little dim sim things that only this family can make, then ask if you feel like seafood, chicken or some other meat. She'll then give you what she thinks you need, and twice as much as anyone should eat at one sitting.'

He smiled at Jess across the table.

'So, tell me what you like,' he said, and smiled suggestively. 'Your preferences?'

Her lips twitched as she wondered what he'd do if she took him up on the hidden meaning in the words, but as she wasn't certain what she liked—except everything about him, and being with him as much as possible—she couldn't have answered anyway.

'Chicken,' she said firmly, her smile widening as his laugh rang out in the small dining room.

'Chicken indeed!' he teased, and she felt the love well up inside her so strongly she wondered she wasn't glowing from its force.

'Talk to me,' she said, when Mrs Lo had put a plate of assorted delicacies in front of them and darted off again. 'Tell me things.'

'Try this first,' he suggested. He lifted a spear of baby corn in his fingers and held the fat end towards her. Something had been wrapped around it and the whole thing seared on a hot plate. 'It's Chinese meets Italian. Baby corn wrapped with prosciutto, then dipped in a fine batter and grilled. Delicious.'

She opened her lips and he fed it to her, excitement knotting her stomach while her taste buds flooded with delight.

'Delicious!' she agreed, letting her tongue touch his fingers as she took the final morsel.

'And dangerous,' he said huskily. 'Perhaps we'd better talk. Choose a subject.'

'You!' she said. 'All about you! Do you know I have no idea how old you are? Not that it matters, but it seems strange.'

He laughed again.

'I'm one up on you there,' he told her. 'I cheated. Looked up your file in the office—which was probably illegal and you can report me if you like—but I'll tell you

I'm five years older than you are, Miss Chapman. I'm thirty. Is that too old for you?'

She felt light-headed with happiness, just being with him. Couldn't stop the smile that played around her lips. But she pretended to consider the question, pursing her mouth and trying to look grave.

'I think thirty is the perfect age,' she said when she felt he'd suffered long enough. 'And now you've confessed to reading my file, you'd better fill me in on what's on yours so we're even.'

It was nonsense talk, arising out of happiness and the tight-coiled anticipatory tension they were both battling to control.

He gave her a potted history—birth date, schooling, university, hospital he'd trained at, one she knew of but hadn't visited. He also told her of his interest in surgery but why, in the end, he'd chosen the country.

'It was odd, really, coming back to Riverview,' he mused.

'Back? You were here before?'

He nodded.

'Not that I remember it clearly, but I'm actually a born and bred Riverviewian. My father's family came from here. He went away to university, met and married my mother, then after a few stints in other areas—he was a teacher— they finally settled in Riverview.'

'Were the girls, your sisters, all born here?' Jess asked, nibbling at a deliciously crisp morsel of prawn toast.

'Not all—and there are only three, not dozens, although it sometimes felt like that. Sue, next to me, was born here, the other two after we'd moved. Since I've returned, and have come to love the place, I keep meaning to ask my parents why they left. I've always had the impression they'd intended making this their home. Then, when I was about four, something happened and they suddenly upped sticks and shifted south to another country town, not unlike Riverview. That's where I grew up—where they still live.'

Jess finished the toast and reached for a prawn encased in paper-fine pastry, then heard a short excerpt of his words repeat themselves in her head. Her mind went into overdrive.

If he'd been four, they'd moved twenty-six years ago.

Before she was born.

The year before she was born?

'What kind of something happened?' she asked, speaking slowly, hiding the dread that clutched her heart with a cold, strangulating force.

It couldn't be. Not possible!

'Something personal, I think,' Andrew told her, shrugging off what might just have been the single most important question she'd ever asked.

'It's not anything I remember, mind you, but an impression—vague memories that a child has of trouble or uncertainty. And it had to have been a sudden decision because it was May, just before my birthday, and I'd been going to have a party and had already asked my friends from kindergarten.'

May made it eight months before she was born!

May was the date on the bus ticket.

It was a coincidence, it had to be. There'd have been hundreds of married men in the town.

Snippets of other conversations rattled in Jess's head. His sisters were all dark. Not unlike her in looks. Andrew's voice explaining that the girls took after his father.

Strong genes.

Jess's stomach churned and she clasped her arms across it, praying the cry of anguish building inside her wouldn't erupt from her lungs.

It was coincidence, she told herself, but it was too late for placatory comments. She had to *know*. She couldn't take the risk it might not be so!

They'd so nearly…

Saved by phone calls!

Until she knew for sure…

'Jessica! What's wrong? Are you sick?'

She stared at Andrew, saw his lips move and his eye-brows draw together as he frowned with concern.

Sick?

She nodded and stood up.

'Stay here,' she said urgently. 'I'll be OK! I need to be alone.'

'Nonsense,' he said gruffly, leaping to his feet so quickly his chair flew backwards and clattered on the floor.

How could she be so aware of noise and movement when the world had just collapsed?

He took her elbow, said something to Mrs Lo, then walked Jess to the door.

She let him take control, knowing her body was too weakened by shock to support itself.

'It must have been the prawn!' he muttered as he stead-ied her along the footpath. 'I've been eating there at least once a week for a couple of years, and never had a bad one. Poor Jess. Are you OK, walking? Would you like to sit somewhere while I go and get the car?'

She could feel his tension, knew he thought she felt ill from the food and was blaming himself for taking her there.

That was fine because there was no way she could blurt out what *had* upset her stomach and made her eyes burn with a pain too deep for tears.

'I'll be all right,' she told him, over and over again. But she knew she might never be all right again.

Ever!

She made it to the house and escaped up the stairs.

'I'm fine,' she said, taking them two at a time. Using different words for the same message. 'Please, Andrew, I just need to be alone.'

She went into the bathroom and washed the silver

shadow off her eyes, cleaned her teeth, then scurried across the hall to her bedroom, where she shut the door, then crawled beneath the bedclothes, curled into a tight ball of misery, and pulled a sheet over her head.

Once hidden from view, she forced the pain from the forefront of her mind and tried to think. Getting out of Andrew's house—that was the first move. She couldn't stay and not explain, yet couldn't leave without a reasonable excuse.

Or could she?

If she didn't tell him?

She could leave a note…

She'd wait until he was asleep, then go. She'd walk back to the cabin at the caravan park and if the rose-giver found her—harmed her—perhaps that would be the best way out of this appalling mess.

Nonsense. There was no way she was going to give in that easily.

First thing in the morning she'd go and visit Mrs Cochrane. Tell her who she was and get the truth about her father.

And if it turned out to be— No, she wouldn't think about that right now!

She curled into a tighter ball as pain swamped her again. She heard the door open and Andrew ask if she needed anything.

'No!' she answered, and heard her despair haunt the word. She added her thanks in a gentler voice, for she truly loved him.

He looked in again, hours later, and she realised it was a final check before he went to bed. She felt him come close to lift the hand she'd left outside the sheet and press his fingers against her pulse.

Had he guessed she was awake?

If he had, he didn't show it—simply satisfied himself she

was alive, then kissed her fingers and walked slowly out of
the room.

She lay in the darkness for another hour, then judged
he'd be asleep. She turned on the bedside light and sighed
as she realised she'd have to pack—again. The small knapsack she'd taken to Sarah's was by the bed, and she retrieved it in the dark and found clean underwear. Her little
toilet bag was on the bureau, kept in the bedroom because
she'd not wanted to leave her clutter in Andrew's bathroom. What else? No work tomorrow, but she wanted to
see Mrs Cochrane. She put in a cotton shift. Spare underwear in case Andrew didn't—wouldn't—bring her case.
And perhaps she'd better take her dirty uniforms so she
could wash them out.

With stiff, fumbling fingers, she packed everything else
into her case and zipped it up, then found a pen and paper
in her handbag.

'I've gone back to the cabin because I need to be alone
for a little while,' she wrote, wondering if it was going to
be more like for ever. 'I would be very grateful if you could
drop my suitcase at the manager's office at the caravan park
when next you're going past.'

It was too stiff, too formal, and she knew he'd find it
hurtful, but what else could she say?

She signed it 'Jessica' then crossed it out and re-signed
'Jess' because that made it less final somehow.

With that done, she straightened the bed and looked
around the room. Chances were she wouldn't have been
sleeping in it much longer anyway! she thought, then shuddered.

Hitching the knapsack over one shoulder and tucking her
handbag under her arm, she went quietly out of the door
and down the stairs, walking through the kitchen and using
the back door, further from Andrew's bedroom, for her escape.

The cabin waited, just as she had left it—perhaps slightly

mustier and dustier. Drained by the emotion of the evening, and the tension of her lonely midnight walk, she collapsed on the bed, registered she'd left her sheets behind and fell into an exhausted slumber.

And hadn't brought a towel. She learned that next morning when she woke, later than she'd hoped, the sun already up and shining brightly. A strange sense of urgency was coursing through her blood. Mrs Cochrane would probably be awake, perhaps already out of bed.

Jess cursed quietly as her original idea had been to offer her help again. But, still, if she could get up there before there were too many people around...

She dried herself on her dirty uniform, dressed in the patterned shift, and, with her stomach grumbling about its lack of sustenance, she headed out of the door.

Her suitcase was standing near the steps, and the thought that Andrew had been and gone made her heart race uncertainly.

Had he been called out during the night?

Or early this morning?

No, she couldn't think about Andrew. Not now. Not yet.

Determination to know, once and for all, who her father was drove her past the case—up the drive, out of the gate and along the footpath towards the hospital.

Later she'd think about other things, get something to eat, work out what to do next with her life.

Later, when she knew one way or the other.

'You're here early this morning for someone not on duty,' Mrs Astbury greeted her as Jess skirted the kitchen, wanting to get to the annexe without delay.

'I wanted to visit my friends back there,' Jess said, and the cook smiled at her.

'You're a kind lass, I'll give you that,' she said, then added something Jess missed as she pressed on towards her destination.

The French doors leading from Mrs Cochrane's room to

the verandah were open, so, knowing the old lady must be awake, she went that way, the words she wanted to say beating in her head.

And pulled up short at the sight of an aide at work, stripping the bed.

'Is Mrs Cochrane in the bathroom?' Jess asked, her manners forgotten in her haste to know the truth.

'Mrs Cochrane?' the young woman echoed. 'Oh, dear, you were friendly with her, weren't you? I'm sorry. You wouldn't have known. She died during the night.'

Jess felt her knees give way and would have pitched forward if the aide hadn't seen her sway and caught hold of her, easing her into a chair and pushing her head between her legs.

'She can't have died!' Jess told her, and heard the echo of despair in the pitch of her voice.

'I'm sorry,' the young woman said, 'but she was very old. Very frail.'

Jess raised her head and looked around.

'Where is she?' she asked, as grief for the grandmother she hadn't known contributed more anguish. 'May I see her?'

The aide looked confused.

'Well, usually the undertaker comes but, with Mrs Cochrane, I think they took her to the morgue here at the hospital. Dr Gilmour said something about an autopsy.'

'Autopsy? They're going to cut her up?' Jess shot out of the chair. 'Where? Where's the morgue?'

She was aware she sounded—and probably looked—demented, but suddenly it seemed sacrilegious that her last piece of family should be so desecrated.

'It's that building at the back of the main hospital,' the aide said. 'It's only routine, I'm sure.'

She sounded puzzled, but Jess had stopped listening, flying out the doors, across the verandah and down to the small brick building she'd assumed was a storage shed of some kind.

Sarah and Andrew were standing outside it, their heads bent as they conversed quietly.

Andrew saw her first and came towards her.

'Jess! You've heard. I'm sorry, I know you'd grown fond of her.'

He put his hand on her shoulder and, although his voice was strained and she knew he would be angry with her for leaving as she had, she felt his love.

It weakened her, but only momentarily.

'The aide said you were going to autopsy her, cut her up. An old lady like that. Do you have to?'

Sarah frowned at her, as if unable to understand her outburst.

'My mother died suddenly,' Jess told her, grasping Sarah's hand in the hope that physical contact might make some difference to her plea. 'She was young, her death so unexpected, they said they had to do it. But Mrs Cochrane? Wouldn't it be natural she'd die in her sleep? Do you have to cut her up? She was such a reserved person, so very private. To do this, it seems so—so invasive!'

'She won't know, Jess,' Andrew said gently, then he nodded to Sarah. 'You go ahead. I'll be with you in a minute.'

He'd been so angry with her, felt so betrayed by her clandestine departure, that he'd not been able to knock on the cabin door for fear the fury might explode out of him. But seeing her like this, shaken, pale with sorrow, he could only put his arm around her shoulders and guide her along the verandah.

'You had no food in the cabin—and ate next to nothing last night,' he said, his voice gruff as he tried to remember his anger but felt only love. 'Go into the kitchen and ask Mrs Astbury to feed you, even if it's only coffee and toast. You'll get sick if you don't eat.'

She looked up at him, her eyes huge in her drawn, white face.

'I had to go,' she said. 'Had to see her. To find out. And now it's too late.'

He shook his head to clear it and tried again to make sense of what she was saying.

Given what Sarah had just told him—

No, not Jess!

'OK, what's happening? No flirting on the job, Dr Kendall.' Helen's voice cut into his internal debate. 'And what are you doing here on your day off, Jessica? Can't stay away from the place?'

'Jessica's had a shock, and she hasn't eaten,' Andrew explained. 'She's not at work, just visiting.'

He let Helen take over, bustling Jess away towards the kitchen, clucking over her in a comforting, motherly fashion.

Far more effective than I'd have been, he thought, still battling anger and plagued by doubts. No! More questions than doubts. He might not have known Jess long, but he had no doubts about her.

He headed back to the morgue where Sarah was setting out the equipment they'd need.

'No helper?'

'There's no one with any experience on duty yet,' she told him. 'You want to do this or shall I?'

'If you've got time, you're welcome to the job,' he said. 'I know you've had infinitely more experience with post-mortems than I have and, if I remember rightly, you've always been challenged by the science of it.'

What worried him was her motivation.

'But tell me again why we're doing it,' he said, thinking of the numerous times he'd signed a death certificate for an elderly patient without considering an autopsy.

'It didn't look right,' Sarah replied. 'Have a look yourself. She's been dead some time, but her face is still blue.'

'That happens in a natural death if she's been gasping, choking perhaps.'

But he knew he was looking for excuses. He could see the blueness, especially around the lips, behind the ears and in her fingernails, sure signs of lack of oxygen in the blood. Yet he wanted it to be a natural death because to consider anything else in connection with an elderly woman made him feel physically ill.

'See her eyelids and here, the tiny petechiae.' Sarah pointed to the pinpoint spots of red on the scalp, signs of minute blood vessels bursting as the patient had struggled to breathe.

'They're signs of asphyxia, Sarah,' he agreed, 'but babies and elderly people have been known to smother accidentally.'

She looked up from sliding a new tape into the recorder.

'Are you asking questions because Jessica made a fuss about an autopsy? Isn't that veering dangerously close to unprofessional behaviour?'

Andrew tried to think clearly and logically, but Jess's disappearance, followed by her words this morning, were like murky shadows in his head.

'Yes, it would be,' he admitted. 'I'm sorry, Sarah. Let's get on with this. I'll assist.' He nodded towards the table. 'But Jess was right. Mrs Cochrane was a very private old lady. She'd hate the indignity of this.'

'She'd hate the indignity of murder as well,' Sarah told him, picking up the camera and starting to take photographs, close-ups of the tiny haemorrhages, asking him to sketch the head and mark in the petechiae.

'She was lying in bed too neatly,' she admitted as she worked. 'That bothered me. Like one of those tests you see in puzzle books. ''What is wrong with this picture?'' Surely if she'd accidentally smothered, she'd have tossed and turned, tangled the blanket or pillow or whatever was across her mouth and nose, until it wound more firmly around her body.'

She pulled out the Polaroid prints and handed them to Andrew to peel and set to dry.

'I spoke to the aide who found her, and she said she hadn't touched a thing. She'd felt for a pulse and, not finding one, called for help. Apparently Mrs Cochrane had made it very clear she wanted no resuscitation attempts when she died. All the staff knew that so I was called in to pronounce her dead.'

'And found what was wrong in the picture?'

'Well, I couldn't believe an old lady would die of asphyxiation lying flat on her back, her head neatly centred on a pillow and with her blankets tucked in around her. Even if she'd choked on something, she'd have moved— at least rumpled the bedclothes and her pillow.'

The flat, unemotional statement made Andrew's blood run cold. He could picture the old lady lying just as Sarah had described, and knew it wasn't right.

Sarah set the camera aside and asked Andrew to help her remove the loose-fitting nightdress. Carl, an orderly deputised to assist, arrived as they finished, and Sarah handed the garment to him, reminding him to put it in a paper evidence bag.

'We have to get it right,' she reminded Andrew, who hadn't realised he'd stiffened until she added the rider.

'Look!' she said, pointing to the mark of a bruise on the bony chest. It was slightly faded, as the blood had drained to settle at the lowest points of the supine body—the back of the head, torso and the underside of the arms and legs.

'A handprint?' Andrew said, coming closer and holding his hand above the mark.

'There won't be prints as she had a full neck-to-knee nightdress on—perhaps a trace of a print on the material, but it's almost impossible to lift them off linen.' Sarah raised the dead woman's right hand and held it in position over the chest, but it was too small to have made the mark, although Andrew's had definitely been too big.

A woman's print?

Why was he lining up the evidence like this?

'It's not our job to either guess or judge,' Sarah reminded him, handing him the camera. He focussed on the discoloration and snapped off a shot as she started dictating her findings into the machine. She picked up a ruler and measured the bruise, its length and breadth, then drew it on a piece of paper and marked the dimensions on that.

Andrew felt ill. How could he not judge when the woman he loved was acting so strangely?

Or should he be judging himself? His love? Didn't his concern show a lack of faith?

'OK, let's turn her over.'

Sarah's command brought his mind back to the job in hand and he set the photographic prints aside to dry and helped her.

The livid marks were shocking against the white skin, but there were no abrasions or contusions to be photographed or listed. Mrs Cochrane had lain on her back for some time after dying—that was all the lividity told them. Something they already knew!

'Have you estimated a time of death?' he asked.

Sarah turned away from the microphone to answer him.

'I was called at six-thirty,' she said. 'One of the staff looked in and then felt something wasn't quite right, so she went closer to check on her.'

'"Felt something wasn't quite right"?' Andrew repeated.

'Well, I'd imagine it was an odour from relaxed sphincter muscles but I'm not putting words in the girl's mouth—just repeating what she said.'

'It's dark at six-thirty. Did she turn on a light?'

Sarah, intent on her external examination, shrugged.

'I have no idea. I guess she must have. Why?'

'If Mrs Cochrane had been sleeping normally, a light would have disturbed her. It seems to me an aide would have been reluctant to do that. Reluctant to turn it on, I mean.'

'You'll have to talk to Rowan about it,' Sarah told him. 'When I got there, the main ceiling light was on and the bedside lamp as well. Her body temperature was down about half a degree Celsius but that's not unusual in an elderly patient, and she was in a warm room, under blankets, so that's not going to be much help for timing the death.'

'Except it's unlikely to have occurred as early as midnight. Even in a warm room the body would have cooled a couple of degrees over six hours.'

'Does midnight have some special significance for you?' Sarah asked, and, although Andrew knew she was making idle conversation, in his heart he'd have preferred Mrs Cochrane to have died before the witching hour.

You can't possibly suspect Jess of murder, a horrified inner voice told him.

You don't know her all that well, another taunted him.

'No,' he said, hiding this internal argument, 'but autopsy reports often seem to feature midnight as a cut-off point. The accident occurred between 6 p.m. and midnight. Or, the deceased was last seen outside the night club at midnight. It almost seems obligatory to have it in there somewhere.'

'Well, it won't be in this one. I'm not rushing into anything, but the lividity isn't very advanced and there's no sign of rigor in the small facial muscles even now, although the warmth of the room would have accelerated rather than delayed it. To me lack of rigor puts it under four hours ago. It's what now? Eight? That makes it after four as far as I'm concerned.'

On Sarah's signal, they again turned the incredibly light body, moving it gently and carefully, allowing the body as much dignity as possible in these undignified circumstances.

Once the internal examination began it was easier, Andrew decided. That was until Sarah dissected carefully beneath the bruised skin on the chest and found osteoporosis-weakened ribs separated from their costal cartilage—a sure sign that force had been applied.

His stomach knotted with futile anger that someone could be so callous.

'Third and fourth ribs damaged,' Sarah dictated, then turned again to Andrew. 'Not that it would have taken much pressure. The bones are showing a serious calcium deficiency. Look, they're almost transparent in places.'

He agreed with her, then again confirmed her findings when she pointed out more petechiae present on the surface of the lungs. Sarah was nothing if not thorough, and she carefully opened the trachea and larynx to make sure there was no obstruction which could have caused the old woman to choke to death. That done, and noted, she lifted out the lungs and trachea, moving on.

Organs were removed, samples taken, slides prepared and carefully labelled, before being packed for transport to the pathology labs at the base hospital.

By the time she reached the head he was expecting to see tiny haemorrhages in the brain, and wasn't disappointed. All the signs of asphyxia were present, and the bruising and cracked ribs made an accident unlikely.

Rowan arrived as Sarah was involved with packaging the specimens and Andrew was carefully sewing up the incisions, apologising silently to the old woman for having had to treat her in this way. She'd been Iain's patient, but he'd been called to see her occasionally and had admired her indomitable spirit. He could understand Jess being attracted to her, for they shared the same inner reserve.

Jess!

'Why am I here? What am I investigating?' Rowan

asked. 'I don't have to be told about every death in town, you know.'

Andrew remembered the stories he'd heard about Caroline Cordell's death and realised the local policeman didn't want another murder on his hands.

'She died of asphyxia—suffocation,' Sarah explained, 'and I would probably have let it go at that, but it felt wrong.' She quickly filled in the details for Rowan, not wanting him to think this could be dismissed as 'woman's intuition'.

'There's a bruising like a palm print on her chest,' Andrew added, backing her up, although Sarah guessed he was hating every minute of this. 'And rib damage.'

'So, how do you see it?' Rowan asked, and Sarah hesitated.

'I don't have to hazard guesses,' she reminded him, 'but Mrs Cochrane was frail. I would think one hand on her chest to hold her down and make it hard for her to breathe deeply, and a pillow held over her head.'

'The hand on her chest had to be applied with considerable force to leave a bruise and affect the ribs,' Andrew commented. 'I mean, it wouldn't have taken long for her to die, but that bruise could only have been made while her heart was still pumping.'

'Could the bruise be older?' Rowan asked. 'Did someone help her bathe? Would one of the nurses up there know if she had it before she went to bed last night?'

'The bruise could be older, but if she'd suffered the rib damage at the same time it would have been very painful,' Sarah told him. 'You might ask if she'd complained of chest pain.'

Rowan nodded to where the cool-boxes were packed ready for transportation to the bigger hospital.

'You want me to take care of that lot?' he asked, and Sarah looked to Andrew for guidance—more backup. They both knew an autopsy could be done within a hospital without involving the law, but in this case there was sufficient evidence of possible foul play to make it a legal matter.

He hesitated for a few seconds then nodded at Rowan.

'I'll go along with Sarah's instincts that it wasn't right,' he told the policeman. 'You can take it from here.'

Sarah stayed to complete the official chain-of-evidence requirements while Andrew departed, muttering to himself about being late on the wards but no doubt to check on Jessica.

He was love-struck, poor man.

Sarah knew she should be pleased for him, but she found herself wishing he'd fallen in love with someone less complicated—someone who wasn't being targeted with roses.

Someone who'd been a little less emotional about the autopsy.

She stopped the thought right there.

Surely not!

Jessica Chapman was a kind, caring and compassionate young woman. She'd been understandably upset by Mrs Cochrane's death.

But she definitely hadn't wanted the autopsy!

CHAPTER EIGHT

FORTIFIED by Helen's blunt kindness and Mrs Astbury's tea, Jess felt better—so much so that when Helen asked if she'd mind doing a couple of hours' work because once again they were short-staffed and it would save her, Helen, phoning around to call someone in, Jess agreed.

'It will have to be in civvies,' she said. 'Like this!'

'You look fine like that,' Helen told her. 'You are a love. If it's any comfort to you, I shouldn't be here either. I don't know how Abby manages!'

Jess smiled and hid her relief. Right now, work was definitely the best option, because she certainly didn't want to go back to the cabin on her own and have to think about what had happened.

She headed for Men's, hoping no one would realise it was only her body going through the motions of her duties. Her mind was way out in some different galaxy, where, instead of air, she was breathing in both pain and confusion.

The little boy who'd lost his tonsils was sitting up in bed, finishing a plate of ice cream.

'It was more a bribe for good behaviour than a necessity,' Cheryl Jones, the sister on duty, told her. 'He'd proved his fitness by eating toast but he's going home later this morning and was getting over-excited at the prospect.'

She glanced around their depleted ward, and added, 'No new customers in here. Do you mind covering Outpatients and being on call for Cas for the next few hours?'

Jess followed her gaze across the empty beds.

'Where's Mr Ambrose?'

Cheryl chuckled.

'He's still here but already up and about, no doubt trying

116

to prove to everyone he's capable of looking after himself if he gets the spare bed in the annexe.'

The casual words reached through to the far galaxy, shocking Jess with their inevitability.

'It seems too soon,' she muttered, and Cheryl laughed again.

'Not to Mr Ambrose it doesn't,' she said jokingly. 'In fact, if they suspect foul play, he'd have to be number one suspect.'

Suddenly the other galaxy wasn't so far away.

'Why would they suspect foul play?' Jess demanded.

Cheryl shrugged.

'Who knows? But Carl was called over to assist with a post,' she said, mentioning the orderly who was usually on duty in the ward. 'Always makes you wonder, if they go to that bother.'

Jess shook her head, denial screaming in her head, although she knew whatever had happened could have no connection to her presence in the town—her mission.

Her thwarted mission!

She heard the bell announcing that someone had arrived for an outpatient appointment, and headed towards the big waiting room. Work had always provided an escape from her emotions. If she concentrated on the job, on every detail of what she was doing, she wouldn't have to think of anything else.

That theory was OK as far as it went—which was when she realised Andrew would also be working in Outpatients.

'Good morning, Mrs Butcher,' she said, glancing around but seeing no evidence that Andrew had arrived for the appointments. 'Come to have your foot dressed?'

It was an easy one. She could do the dressing herself and not involve Andrew.

'Yes, I need the dressing but first I want to show it to Andrew. That's why I didn't let the home nursing service do it today. It's not healing right and he'll know what to do. When Mrs Carter had her bunions done, they were better far faster than this.'

While the garrulous woman ran through a précis of 'bunions she had known', Jess stripped off the old dressings and examined the healing wound. Leaving it with no dressing would be better, but perhaps if Mrs Butcher didn't have the daily contact of the nursing service, she'd miss it, be lonely without the regular visitor.

Mrs Cochrane had been lonely.

'There's a fine line between pandering to them and doing what's best for the whole person, particularly with regard to their mental health,' Andrew said a little later, when they'd reassured Mrs Butcher, put on fresh, dry dressings and seen their patient off. 'Depression is such an insidious thing, particularly as people age.'

Jess knew he was talking about work for the same reason she was trying to submerge herself in it—to stop thinking other thoughts. Earlier he'd scolded her for agreeing to the extra duty, though she sensed he wasn't unhappy to have her where he could keep an eye on her.

She agreed, trying to concentrate on his theories, but even fear of the forbidden couldn't negate the physical symptoms of her love for him, or stop the waves of attraction bombarding her body.

Until he brushed against her and she leapt away!

'Who's next?' he asked.

She heard the crispness in his voice and saw the hurt in his eyes, but not knowing made it impossible to explain her behaviour. How could she raise the spectre of guilt where maybe none existed? She couldn't. Couldn't set such an unpredictable and potentially destructive force in motion.

'There's a croupy baby just come into Cas. I put them in the small treatment room and started a humidifier. There are no outpatient appointments until eleven-thirty when a Mr Young is coming in to have a basal cell carcinoma excised. And your tonsillectomy is waiting for you to discharge him. Cheryl said his mother is coming up at ten or ten-thirty.'

He glanced at his watch.

'She'll be here already, but I'd better see the baby first before I tackle young Gary. I'll go through to Women's after that, so you'll find me there if I'm needed.'

The green eyes met hers as he said the last word. They were more questioning than accusatory, but still wary. Pained.

I *do* need you, she wanted to say, but couldn't.

'I'll do the BCC in the bigger treatment room, so if you could set up a tray for me in there.'

His politeness cut her more sharply than a scalpel, but she welcomed the pain as it shifted the focus off her own inner agony.

'You'd better come with me to see the baby. Keep an eye on the mother, maybe get her a cup of tea. She's sure to be upset.'

Jess followed him, thinking how he'd offered her tea earlier—the quick fix, the panacea for all ills in this country. Have a cuppa and everything will be all right.

Only it wouldn't work this time, would it?

For the baby's mother, though, perhaps it would.

The morning rolled on, a young school teacher the first admission, Andrew diagnosing pneumonia and opting to keep him in hospital to ensure the order for bed rest was enforced over the weekend.

'Silly young fool,' Andrew had muttered as he wrote up an admission form. 'If I send him home and he begins to improve, I wouldn't put it past him to play football tomorrow.'

'I thought it was just a bad dose of the flu,' the patient, Giles Cameron, explained to Jess. He'd been tucked into bed in hospital-issue pyjamas and his flatmate alerted to bring up his personal belongings. 'But the home ec. teacher kept saying I shouldn't be at school if I was contagious and insisted I get up here and onto some antibiotics.'

'Next time you might see a doctor earlier,' Jess chided, as the young man, weakened by so much explanation, lay back against his pillows and smiled wanly at her.

She left him to go back to Outpatients where she'd be assisting with the BCC—or watching, perhaps passing instruments, holding dressings, then clearing up the mess later.

Clearing up the mess later was easy but standing next to Andrew while he cut and stitched was less bearable.

'I'll leave these slides for the pathology courier, then I'm going home,' he announced when the patient had departed and Jess was on her knees, picking up the bits of packaging that had fallen to the floor. 'I don't suppose there's any point in telling you I'm concerned about you living in the cabin on your own.'

She nodded, meaning she knew he was concerned, then shook her head because she didn't want him thinking she'd go back to live with him.

He walked away, his back stiff with anger, and sadness swamped her as she watched him go.

It was better this way, she told herself, but the words had a very hollow ring to them, and her heart ached with sudden loneliness.

'Rowan Crane wants to see you. He's in the admin office.'

Cheryl came bustling into the treatment room as Jess disposed of the needle and scalpel blade in the sharps bin. She was obviously bursting with curiosity, but Jess had as little idea as she did why the policeman would want her.

After all, no one knew!

'I guess because I used to visit Mrs Cochrane. I was there last night, although I left before she had dinner so other people must have seen her and spoken to her after me.'

'Carl says it could be murder!' Cheryl whispered. 'Says she was smothered by a pillow!'

Every cell in Jess's body seemed to freeze, and her own voice came echoing back to her. The night they'd had dinner with Sarah. Joking about Mr Ambrose and murder. How had she phrased her suggestion? Something about smothering being undetectable? Had she mentioned a pillow?

'Carl shouldn't talk,' she said weakly, then she dragged her feet out of the room, wondering if this was just routine or if either Sarah or Andrew had mentioned that silly conversation to the police.

She walked along the verandah towards the office, not exactly dawdling but not hurrying, looking out across the grounds towards the river, hoping a little of the peace and tranquillity of the surroundings would seep into her soul.

The office door was open, and she could see Rowan's large frame settled, apparently comfortably, in the chair behind the desk.

Jess smiled at him as she walked in, then realised he wasn't alone in the room. Andrew was there, lounging back against a filing cabinet, his arms folded across his chest.

'I've explained to Rowan that as the medical officer in charge of the hospital I should be present while he talks to staff.'

Jess didn't buy the story. He was doing his protective thing and she wasn't sure if she should be grateful or annoyed.

'Are you talking to all the staff?' she asked Rowan.

'All who had dealings with Mrs Cochrane,' he told her. 'Staff at the annexe tell me you visited her regularly.'

He's asking why, Jess realised, but she contented herself with answering, 'Yes.'

'For any particular reason?' Rowan asked. 'I mean, why her? She wasn't what you'd call the world's most cheerful soul.'

'Perhaps that's why,' Jess said, wondering if an evasion constituted lying where the police were concerned. 'In the beginning, I spent quite a lot of time with Bob, and in groups of other residents, but with Mrs Cochrane...'

Jess glanced at Andrew but his face was impassive. Probably thinking he'd rather be at home!

'She didn't have any other visitors. She seemed lonely, seemed to like my visits.'

'She didn't have any other visitors because she'd been rude to just about every person in this town,' Rowan told her. 'And the ones she hadn't offended hated her for her behaviour towards her daughter, although I doubt if anyone knows the truth of that story. I was too young to remember it, but apparently she was there one day and gone the next with no word of explanation. Of course, more than one person claimed the old lady had murdered her and buried her in the back garden.'

He scratched his head.

'I guess I'll have to do something about finding her— the daughter. Let her know her mother's dead. I wonder if the old trout left her the money, or if some cat's home will be the beneficiary.'

He wrote a note to himself in his notebook, then looked up at Jess again.

'Are you OK?' he asked.

She nodded, battling to regain the control his words about 'the daughter' had destroyed. She wanted to yell at him, tell him her mother had been a person in her own right, a warm, loving, tender, wonderful woman.

Not 'the daughter'.

It had also been her cue to explain a few things, but she couldn't. Not yet. Maybe not ever.

'So, you visited her last night? What time?'

Jess sorted her thoughts into order. 'I finished work a little late. It must have been about five by the time I went up to the annexe.' She glanced at Andrew. 'We went home about six, didn't we?'

As soon as the question was spoken she regretted it, hearing the intimacy that no longer existed echoing in the words.

Andrew seemed unperturbed. He nodded to confirm the time, cool now, no longer angry.

She shivered but told herself it was for the best.

'And you didn't see her after that? Didn't come back later? Presumably, since you're staying with Andrew, you've an alibi for the rest of the night.'

'Alibi?'

Disbelief had her on her feet, her arms flung out to emphasise the question.

'Why would I need an alibi? Why would you think I'd killed her? I liked her, liked talking to her...' Had needed to talk to her just once more!

She slumped back into the chair as frustration and despair overwhelmed all other feelings.

'If you've no other questions for Jessica...'

Andrew's voice pierced the fog, a steely quality in it alerting Jess to the fact that he was even more upset than he'd been earlier.

Why?

Because she hadn't answered Rowan's question? And, in not answering, let the policeman think she'd been with Andrew all night? Implicating Andrew in the lie?

She turned towards him, wondering what he thought— what he'd say if she let the misconception ride. His face was so devoid of expression he might have been wearing a mask. A mask that hid him from her, cut her off, and left her floundering in an abyss of uncertainty.

'I wasn't at Andrew's.'

She blurted out the words, ashamed she'd let the lie sit around as long as it had.

'I went back to the cabin at the caravan park. After all, there'd been no roses for a day or so, no problems.'

No problems? That was a laugh. She might re-visit it later when she needed one. But right now Rowan was regarding her with renewed interest.

About to pounce.

'And you were there alone all night?'

Jess nodded. Now it was out she found she didn't really care what happened.

'And this morning? Did anyone see you leave the park?'

She shook her head but before she could answer Andrew intervened.

'Why these questions, Rowan?' he demanded. 'I can understand you needed to talk to Jess because she visited the old lady last night and might have noticed if she was upset or worried over something, but to be asking for an alibi? I agree with Jess. Why the hell should she need one?'

He felt wrung out. He'd run the full gamut of his emotions today, beginning with shock, and disappointment, and anger, when he'd woken to find Jess had disappeared. Since then he'd battled suspicion, doubt, more anger than he believed possible, pity, love and anger once again. He felt shredded, torn apart, destroyed.

And furious with Rowan who was burbling on about routine.

'It's not routine,' he countered. 'You haven't asked me where I was last night, or Helen, or any other staff. Why Jess? If she's under some kind of cloud in your mind, she should be talking to a solicitor, not you.'

'I wasn't thinking of Jessica as a suspect,' Rowan argued, 'but trying to trace her movements because of the person who's been pestering her. I mean, who'd kill an old lady except someone who had something to gain from her death or someone who's not right in the head? And it's unlikely we'd have two nutters in town at the same time.'

Andrew saw Jess tremble at the assertion and wanted to

hold her in his arms, in spite of what she'd done. He stayed where he was, knowing that holding her wouldn't be enough.

Knowing also that Rowan wasn't being entirely truthful. Beneath the plausible excuse he was considering that, until Jess's arrival in Riverview, there'd been no trouble. He had her firmly pegged as a possibility for the 'someone not right in the head' award.

'Mr Ambrose gets a bed in the annexe,' he told Rowan. 'He had something to gain. Did you question him?'

'I'll eventually question everyone in the hospital,' the policeman replied, pocketing his pen and notebook. 'Will you feel obliged to be in on all the interviews?'

It was a challenge Andrew knew he had to meet.

'I would hope you'll do the hospital the courtesy of having a senior staff member present at all of them,' he responded. 'I'd consider Linda at the annexe suitable, and Helen or one of the sisters down here.'

'I'll be in touch,' Rowan said, and Andrew didn't miss the warning in his voice.

Andrew didn't say goodbye to Rowan either, being too concerned about Jessica who was huddled in the chair looking very small and desperately unhappy.

'It's because you're new to town,' he said, kneeling beside the chair so he could look into her face. 'In small towns people would always prefer any miscreant to be a stranger. It's so much easier than having to live with the fact that someone they knew, and probably liked, did something wrong.'

She pushed back her heavy hair, which had fallen forward, and looped it behind her ears. Then, the full misery in her face revealed, she looked deep into his eyes.

'It's going to get worse,' she whispered, and an icy chill began in his guts and spread outwards through his body.

He tried to argue, to deny it, but the words wouldn't

come, then she lifted her hand and brushed her fingers lightly down his cheek.

'Stay clear of me, Andrew,' she said, her voice husky but the warning clear. 'Don't let this nastiness and suspicion touch you. If it does it will affect your career, your future in the town you love.'

'You're my future,' he told her, as the love he felt did battle with the cold, and the beginning of an inner warmth told him it had won.

'I can't be,' she said, the words little more than a ragged sigh. 'Or might not be able to be. I don't know. I thought I could find out, but now it's too late. So keep away. Please, Andrew? Please, stay away from me, my love!'

He heard her desperation, but the words made no sense. He moved, wanting to hold her, to touch her skin, her shining hair.

She shrank back and when he saw her recoil from him, as if he'd intended harm, it hurt him more than all the words she'd spoken. Anger returned, a raging fury, directed more at fate than Jess, but she was there, and tangible, and fate wasn't.

'I can't pretend to understand what's going on,' he said, straightening up, 'but should you ever care to explain you know where I live.'

He stormed out of the office, barrelled into Helen, who was coming in, and said, 'I don't want Rowan Crane talking to any employee of this hospital without a senior staff member present. See to it, will you?' He kept going, knowing she'd be standing, staring after him, her mouth agape.

In his two and a half years' tenure at the hospital he'd never roared out orders or treated any staff member as an underling, there to do his bidding.

Well, he thought grimly, striding down towards his car, perhaps it was time for a change. Time to say, No more Mr Nice Guy! Time to get some action around this place.

By the time he started the engine he was smiling at the

thought, but he knew the smile was only on the surface. Underneath his skin there was an uncertainty so deep he was being sucked down into it—in danger of being whirled into its vortex and drowning in it.

Jess sat in the chair, too numb, too depleted by emotion, to move.

'What on earth's got into Andrew?' Helen demanded, striding into the room and coming to an abrupt halt in front of Jess. She remained immobile long enough for Jess to realise she expected a reply.

'I upset him by shifting back to the cabin,' she said, hoping a small portion of the truth would satisfy Helen. 'He's concerned about me being there on my own.'

'And so he should be,' Helen told her. 'You were much better off with him. I hope you didn't do it because you were worried about what people might think. He's got broad shoulders, Andrew. He could bear the load.'

Jess smiled at this championing of the man she loved.

'I know all that,' she said, and pushed herself stiffly out of the chair.

'Look at you!' Helen scolded. 'You're exhausted. I've found a nurse willing to start a split shift at two. And as we're getting rid of Mr Ambrose and Men's only has one patient, I'm sure we can manage. Thanks for filling in, but you can go off home now. Get some rest. You look like a washed-out dishrag, poor child!'

Helen waved her hands in a shooing motion, and Jess, more tired than she'd realised until she'd had to bear her weight, didn't argue.

'I'll just tell Cheryl,' she said.

'No,' Helen said. 'Get going. I'll tell Cheryl.' She hesitated, then said, 'Wait a sec. Have you got a phone in that cabin?'

Jess shook her head, wondering what phones had to do with her going home or telling Cheryl.

Helen rummaged around on her desk and produced a mobile.

'Here,' she said. 'Take this. It's an old one we used for on-call staff. Abby replaced the analogues with digitals before she went on leave, so there are spares hanging around. At least, if you get a scare, you can phone someone.'

Grateful for the bluff kindness, Jess thanked her, took the phone and departed, trudging down the steps and across the car park, making for the footpath that led to the caravan park.

She stopped at the little shop attached to the park office and felt in the pocket of her shift to see if she had any money. Yes! Ten dollars. Finally something was going her way. She silently congratulated herself for making a habit of folding some money into her pocket when she went out for a walk. It could have been there for a week, but now she bought teabags, milk, bread and butter with it, then added honey as an afterthought, thinking the sweetness might help.

'They get the bloke leaving the flowers?' Rob asked her, as she paid for her purchases.

'No, but they will,' she said, and walked away, so weary, now she was close to her temporary home, that she had trouble putting one foot in front of the other.

Her suitcase was still outside the door.

She frowned at it, debated lifting it inside, then shook her head.

Later! Right now she wanted to fall on the bed and sleep for about a century.

It wasn't quite that long, but four hours' sleep made her feel almost human again.

Unhappy still, but that was part of being human.

She showered, then realised she still had no towel. She dried herself on her uniform again, pulled on the blue shift she'd worn the previous night and again considered her choices. Should she make a cup of tea and have something to eat before or after she retrieved her suitcase? She opted for before, but while she waited for the kettle to boil she ran water in the hand basin in the little bathroom and soaked both her uniforms.

'Tomorrow's Sunday. You could have washed tomorrow!' The chiding reminder, spoken aloud to chase away the emptiness, made her feel slightly better. She had a full day off before she had to face Andrew again. One day to think and plan, to work out how she could discover what she needed to know and put whatever she came up with into action.

The thought of action cheered her, and she drank her tea, ate her honey sandwich, then opened the door and went out to get the suitcase. She'd make the bed and put her little personal things around so the cabin became homely again.

For some reason the thought of 'homely' made her think of Andrew's photo albums, looking through them with him, laughing as he'd related tales about his childhood.

'Oh, Andrew,' she whispered, wishing she had just one of those photos now to put beside the treasured print of her mother and herself at her graduation.

'Well, at least I've still got that,' she said, carrying the suitcase inside and heaving it up on the bed. She laid it down flat, unzipped the sides and, still thinking of the photo and her mother, opened the lid.

The smell assailed her first, or perhaps she registered it first because her senses worked automatically. Her eyes had undoubtedly relayed a message to her head, but her mind was refusing to process what they saw.

She heard a cry and knew it was her own, then her legs gave way and she crumpled to the floor, her body pitching forward so her head landed on top of the crushed and faded blossoms and the thorns dug into her skin.

You will not pass out! she told herself, grasping at the tattered threads of consciousness and willing the terror away. She lifted her head and saw, beyond the suitcase, the

mobile phone Helen had insisted she take. She reached out
for it as if to a lifeline, and grasped it in her trembling
fingers.

Who to call?

Not Andrew!

Call the police. Get Rowan here.

And face his questions, his suspicions, on your own?

No, not Rowan. Not yet.

Her heart wanted Andrew, but she knew that wasn't an
option. For one thing he'd insist she shift back in with him.

Sarah?

She focussed on the phone and pressed the numbers for
the hospital, surprised her brain was working well enough
to recall the number. She asked to be put through to the
flat and then, when Sarah answered, the tears she didn't
know she'd been holding back flooded out, and all she
could do was gasp out the doctor's name.

'Jessica? Is that you?' Sarah's voice was shrill with
alarm. 'Where are you? At Andrew's house?'

'At the cabin,' she managed to say, swiping at the tears
that continued to stream down her cheeks.

'Are you in danger? Do you need the police?'

Did she?

No!

She took a deep breath, knowing she needed to convince
Sarah not to call them.

'I'm not in danger,' she said, 'but could you come,
Sarah? Please!'

'I'll be right there,' Sarah said crisply, then Jess heard
the click as she put the phone down.

Still clutching the phone in one hand, she remained on
the floor, her back to the bed so she couldn't see the
crushed roses.

A car pulled up and a door slammed, then Sarah was
beside her, kneeling on the floor.

'Are you hurt?' she demanded.

Jess shook her head.

'Not in pain? Ill?'

Another head-shake, then she shuddered, and Sarah put strong arms around her and helped her to her feet.

'Come and sit out here,' she suggested, guiding Jess, half carrying her, towards the little dinette at the far end of the cabin. 'I'll get you a hot drink then you can tell me all about it.'

'You should look! You have to see them,' Jess told her, baulking at the doorway between the bedroom and the living area. 'In the suitcase, Sarah. I opened it and there they were!'

Sarah listened to the weak insistence in Jessica's voice and, puzzled by what she was to look at, turned back towards the bedroom.

What she'd vaguely assumed to be clothes when she'd rushed to the younger woman's side now morphed into roses, massed across the top of the case.

Crushed and dying beauty.

'Oh, sweet heaven!' she muttered, getting Jess to the seat at the other end of the cabin then abandoning her as she went back to the bedroom to take a closer look. 'Has someone been in here? Was the case inside?'

She glanced back at Jess, who shook her head, her fear now becoming weariness or, worse, exhaustion.

'Andrew left it outside this morning on his way to the hospital.'

Sarah frowned at her. 'You're not connecting Andrew with any of this, are you?' she asked.

Another head-shake in reply, then a shrug.

'I don't know any more, Sarah,' Jess admitted. 'No, I hadn't connected Andrew with it. I don't think he'd do this to me but, now you mention it, there *are* roses in his garden, aren't there?'

'Not this many!' Sarah told her, refusing to believe the Andrew she knew could harm anyone, let alone a woman he so obviously loved. She picked up a couple of the blooms. 'Anyway, they seem quite fresh—squashed, but not dead enough to have been packed in there since early morning.'

'The suitcase has been outside all day. I came home early this afternoon but slept for hours. I didn't hear anyone about, but the park manager knew I was here. I'm sure he'd have kept an eye out for strangers.'

'It might not be a stranger,' Sarah told her, lifting another rose and then seeing a note. She glanced across at Jess and realised that the other woman had seen the flowers and panicked, then had made the phone call, without having investigated the offerings.

'We should phone Rowan.'

Jess nodded.

'I know we should.' She looked at Sarah. 'I knew that all along but couldn't face him on my own.'

Sarah heard the strength returning to her voice, and decided she'd have to know.

'There's a note beneath the flowers,' she said. 'Do you want to look at it?'

Even from a distance she saw the shudder that ripped through Jess's light frame, noticed the white line around her lips, the greyness in her skin.

'What does it say?' Jess whispered.

Sarah leaned closer, not wanting to touch it in case she tainted the evidence.

'It's to Kristie again,' she said, trying to keep her voice even, although her own tension was coiled so tightly her bones ached. 'It says, ''She shouldn't have made you cry''!'

A sighing sound was all she heard as Jess fainted, sliding off the chair to land in a crumpled heap on the floor.

CHAPTER NINE

SARAH'S training dictated that she attend the patient first, so, oblivious to evidence, she moved the suitcase from the bed to the small dining table, then shifted Jess, now conscious but very shaky, to the bed.

She wrapped the bedcover around Jess's shaking body, then found a blanket in a wardrobe and added that. She boiled water and made a cup of tea, adding a spoon of honey to it before pressing it into Jess's hands and ordering her to drink it.

When she was satisfied that the younger woman had recovered sufficiently she settled herself on the end of the bed and studied her.

'Do you want to talk to me about this before I call Rowan?'

Jess's dark head bobbed up and down.

'Will we begin with the note?'

Evidently not, she realised as Jess paled again, then shook her head with a vehemence that puzzled Sarah. After all, it was the note which had made the other woman faint!

'OK!' she said, not wanting to push. 'Let's start with why you're here—why you suddenly left Andrew's place.'

'I can't tell you that part,' Jess answered. 'Not because I wouldn't give my right hand to talk to someone about it, Sarah, but because it's only a suspicion, and if I mention it and it's wrong, it could hurt so many other people.'

Sarah found herself smiling.

'That doesn't usually stop folk spreading gossip, innuendo and suspicion,' she said, remembering the pain it had once caused her.

'It will stop me,' Jess told her, and Sarah admired her for that at least.

'OK, so we won't talk about that either—what else is there?'

Jess frowned at her, then shrugged.

'Not much else.' Her eyes were filled with such despair that Sarah shifted so she could put her arm around her.

'So we're back to the note,' she said gently. 'Who made you cry?'

She felt Jess tremble, then control the physical reaction, as if willing her body to behave.

'I can't believe the note said that,' she whispered, as if afraid they might be overheard. 'And she didn't make me cry—not deliberately. It was something she said, the way she said it. I was tired, and it affected me.'

'Who is "she", Jess?' Sarah asked, although an uneasiness in her stomach suggested she already knew the answer.

'Mrs Cochrane,' Jess whispered. 'It was Thursday morning, after I'd spent the night at your place. Remember, I went up to the annexe early.' She turned so she could look into Sarah's eyes, perhaps needing to emphasise what she was saying. 'She didn't *make* me cry!' she repeated.

'I have to phone Rowan,' Sarah told her. 'He has to know about this, see the roses and the note, possibly take the suitcase away.'

'I know!' Jess muttered. 'I know you do.'

She eased herself off the bed and made for the bathroom, while Sarah dialled Information and asked to be connected to the local police station.

'Thank goodness you're there,' she said when Rowan answered. 'Could you come over to the caravan park—the last cabin on the left? I'm here with Jessica Chapman. There's something you should see.'

She rang off and listened to splashing noises in the bathroom, thinking through what they'd talked about—and what hadn't been asked or explained.

The bathroom door opened and Jess poked her head out.

'Could you pass me a couple of hangers from that wardrobe?' she asked. 'Heaven knows why, but I started to wash my uniforms earlier. I've just rinsed them out and I can hang them in the shower recess to drip.'

Sarah passed the coat-hangers, and guessed that doing something so ordinary was making Jess feel better, anchoring her to reality perhaps.

She waited until Jess rejoined her, then asked the question that had occurred to her only minutes earlier. 'Who saw you crying?'

Jess stared at Sarah, unable to believe she hadn't considered this herself. The scene obligingly recreated itself in her mind, her flight from the room, across the verandah and down towards the hospital.

For a fleeting moment she relished the memory of Andrew's strong arms around her, then, in case even a memory might betray her, or him, she banished it.

'I suppose anyone who was near the annexe or out the back of the hospital could have seen me and noticed I was upset,' she said, 'but I wasn't in any state to take notes.'

She thought Sarah's sudden stillness meant she suspected a lie, then she heard the noise of a car door slam.

'Rowan? That was quick.'

Sarah moved towards the door and opened it, peering out then standing back to let in, not Rowan, but Andrew.

Ignoring Sarah, he headed straight towards Jess.

'If you insist on staying here alone, you'd better have this,' he said, and thrust another mobile phone towards her. 'I've stuck a list of numbers on the back of it—the police, the hospital, Sarah's flat.' He paused, then added gruffly, 'Mine!'

Jess took it and held it tightly in her hand. It was brand new. He'd done this for her. Some repayment for the suspicious thoughts she'd harboured about him a few minutes earlier!

'Thank you,' she said, but he'd already turned away and was making for the door, apparently intent on leaving.

'What the hell is this?' He lunged towards the suitcase as he roared out his demand, but Sarah moved more quickly, stepping in front of him.

'Don't touch it. Rowan's on his way. Jess found the roses there when she opened it.'

He swung back to face Jess.

'And you contacted Sarah?' he said flatly.

She saw pain flare in his eyes and heard it tighten his voice, but couldn't save him from it. Much as she'd wanted his support, she *had* phoned Sarah.

'Why?' he demanded. 'Am I a suspect? Have you twigged to the fact that I grow roses in my garden? Added two and two to make a hundred and five?'

He glared at her, daring her to answer him, but Sarah defused the tension by touching his arm and saying, 'Whoever did it left another note. Addressed to Kristie.'

The distraction worked and he swung back to Sarah.

'Where? Let me see it?'

Again she stopped him.

'Hey, go steady, friend. Anger isn't going to help us sort this out.'

'Damn him, and damn his Kristie. You know the only Kristie anyone's come up with is some woman on a TV drama and she's dead anyway.'

Jess heard the words, and saw his face go hard as if their meaning had suddenly frightened him. He crossed back to where she was standing in the doorway, still holding the phone in her hands, and rested his hands on her shoulders.

'That was a stupid thing to say,' he apologised. 'You will not come to any harm, I promise you that. And if you won't come back and live at my place, then I'll sleep outside your door, take leave if necessary to follow you around until whoever is doing this to you is caught.'

Then, taking advantage of Jess's willpower being weakened by this declaration, he pulled her into his arms and held her close to his body.

Jess knew she should move away, tell him it was wrong, but it felt so right and it was only for a minute. With Sarah there and Rowan on the way, nothing could come of it. She rested her head on his shoulder and sighed.

Another car door slammed and she moved away from the sanctuary of Andrew's arms to watch Sarah usher Rowan in and point towards the case.

He looked but didn't touch, peering closer to read the note which Jess still hadn't seen but assumed was buried in the roses.

He asked the questions Sarah had asked—about the case, where it had been and when.

'I left it outside the door at about seven this morning. I didn't knock because I didn't want to disturb Jessica,' Andrew responded.

'I didn't notice it until I was on my way over to the hospital, and I left it there because I couldn't be bothered taking it inside,' Jess added. 'Then, when I got home, I was tired—had a sleep, a cup of tea. I suppose it was close to six by the time I went out and brought it in.'

'She phoned me when she opened it.' Sarah put in her tuppence-worth. 'At about six.'

'It was closer to seven when you phoned me,' Rowan said, and Sarah glared at him.

'Jess was in shock. The roses weren't going anywhere. It was more important to look after her than to get you here immediately. After all, whoever did it could have fiddled with the case any time after seven this morning. He would hardly be still hanging around now.'

Jess watched Rowan's face and guessed he wasn't too

impressed by this reasoning. Then, as if attracted by her scrutiny, he turned to her.

'Was the case locked? Is anything missing?'

She stared blankly at him for a moment, then realised it hadn't occurred to her to check her belongings.

'It wasn't locked—it zips closed and if it ever had a key it's been lost for ages.'

'And we didn't want to touch anything until you came,' Sarah put in. 'So she wouldn't know if anything is missing.'

'Well, you'd better have a look now,' Rowan suggested. 'Wait until I get rid of these.'

He disappeared outside, returning with a large plastic bag and an envelope. Using tweezers, he lifted the note from its scented bed and slid it into the envelope.

'Hold the bag for me, Andrew,' he suggested, and Andrew moved closer and held the bag open while Rowan lifted the roses one by one and dropped them in.

'Fourteen,' he said, as if the number was important. He took the bag from Andrew and sealed it across the top. 'First thing in the morning, I'll send someone up to see what's been cut in the hospital garden.'

'But so many people cut the roses,' Sarah objected. 'I cut a fresh one every day or so to keep in my room, the aides pick them for the wards, the women in the annexe who look after the gardens are always taking a bunch back up there.'

'I can still try to match these to the bushes,' Rowan insisted, then he turned to Andrew. 'And to yours,' he warned, and Andrew nodded.

'I'd expect you to,' he said. 'Not that they'll match. Mine are all what Abby calls tea roses and, while I might not know much about the species, I do know they don't look like this.'

'But you have equal access to the hospital rose garden,' Rowan pointed out, and Jess wondered if he was teasing

Andrew for some reason, or if he was really suspecting the hospital's medical officer of involvement.

It made her feel uneasy, so much so that she stepped forward and stood beside the man she loved.

'I don't believe Andrew would do this to me,' she said firmly.

Rowan didn't reply, asking instead, 'What's this in the note about someone making you cry?'

It wasn't a question she welcomed but at least he was leaving Andrew alone, although Andrew had stiffened in such a way she doubted whether he approved of the conversational switch.

'The note was addressed to Kristie, not me,' Jessica reminded the policeman.

'What did it say?' Andrew demanded.

Jess kept quiet, and prayed Rowan would as well, but Sarah had no inhibitions.

'It *was* addressed to this Kristie person,' she confirmed. 'And it said, "She shouldn't have made you cry."'

'But that's tantamount to an admission of murder!' Andrew stormed, and the words hung in the air above their heads, doom-laden. Fear descended slowly like a settling cloud.

'What do you mean?' Rowan demanded. 'Who made someone cry?'

He glared at Jess. 'Could this apply to you even though you're not this Kristie person? Whoever's writing the notes obviously thinks you are. When did you cry?'

All last night? Most of today? Inside, not obviously, but crying none the less.

She couldn't answer, couldn't say words that would immediately implicate Andrew.

Sarah answered for her.

'I asked that,' she told Rowan. 'Apparently she was upset after seeing Mrs Cochrane on Thursday morning. She left the annexe in tears and anyone could have seen her.'

Rowan's attention swung back to focus on Jess.

'Forget about who saw you. Who did *you* see, Jessica?'

She opened her lips but the name wouldn't come.

Andrew rescued her, moving back to put an arm around her shoulders.

'She saw me. I was there. She raced across from the annexe to the hospital and ran into me. But there could have been any number of other people about—nursing staff, aides, orderlies. It was just before eight—change of shift, people coming on duty.'

'At the back of the hospital?'

Rowan's sarcasm frightened Jess even more than the implications of the note. He was looking for a suspect, and Andrew fitted.

'But I'm not Kristie!' she said firmly. 'Surely that's the crux of the whole thing. Whoever is doing this is doing it to her, not me, so if we find out who she is, and if she cried, we'll know more.'

Rowan nodded, but Jess guessed he wasn't convinced.

'Did you ever ask Mrs Cochrane about this Kristie?' he asked, shocking Jess so much that she again had trouble answering.

'Why on earth would I do that? I barely knew her. I used to read to her at night, sit with her for a while, talk to her occasionally.'

'Why?'

Andrew's statement had been doom-laden, but the policeman's question was an even worse herald of disaster. Jess hesitated and looked at Sarah, who was waiting for an answer, and at Rowan, who was now frowning at her, and then at Andrew.

'May I speak to you alone?' she said to Rowan.

'No!'

The word was torn from Andrew's throat, fear for Jessica shaking the very foundations of his being.

'Don't do anything stupid, Jess,' he pleaded. 'Think this

through. Talk to a solicitor. Don't incriminate yourself in something you didn't do.'

She turned to him and actually smiled, totally oblivious of where Rowan's questions were leading. He guessed she thought she was protecting him, but he was innocent anyway.

And wasn't she?

Didn't he believe in her?

How could he not, loving her as he did?

'Let's not overdo the drama, Andrew,' Rowan warned, 'and, yes, we'll talk, Jessica. But first, now we've got the roses out, could you look through your case and see if anything's missing?'

Andrew watched her straighten, then walk towards the suitcase. He could see her tension in the way she moved, feel her fear in the air around her.

'You packed late at night,' he reminded her, hoping to chase away a little of her apprehension. 'You could have left things at my place.'

She shot a half-smile at him and he silently applauded her courage as she lifted out the garments one by one and stacked them on the table. Silence fell between them, as if all the energy in the room was now focussed on those slim, methodically moving hands.

They fluttered now, feeling inside the empty case, riffling again through the clothes, not methodically at all this time, pulling open the soft material in the lid to search again.

'The photo's gone,' she whispered, looking towards Rowan, then Sarah and finally to him. 'A photo of my mother and myself on my graduation day. It was in here, I know it was. I always pack it first, wrapped in clothes so the glass doesn't break.'

He thought back, knowing he'd looked around the room to see if any trace of Jess had been left—apart from the suitcase.

'It could be back at the house,' he suggested, although he knew it wasn't.

'Why don't you go and look for it?' Rowan said to him. 'Take Sarah with you while I talk to Jessica.'

Andrew knew it was an order, although it didn't sound like one, but he wasn't going to obey if Jess needed him.

Nor, apparently, was Sarah.

'Would that be all right with you?' she asked Jess, who nodded and dredged up a wan but grateful smile for Sarah.

'What the hell is going on here?' Sarah asked, as soon as they were clear of the cabin.

'I've no idea,' Andrew said, 'but if that woman murdered the old lady, I should be taken out and shot—put down—because my judgement of human nature is so faulty I'm a risk to all humanity.'

'No one knows what people are capable of,' Sarah reminded him. 'What we'd do ourselves in certain circumstances.'

'I know what I'd like to do when I find whoever's behind this!' Andrew muttered, opening the passenger door of his car for Sarah and waiting for her to settle into the seat before shutting it with rather too much force.

'What I'd like to do is talk to Abby,' Sarah told him, when he got in behind the wheel.

'Talk to Abby? Where does she come into this?'

He started the car and drove slowly out of the park.

'It's the Kristie business that bothers me. And Jessica reminded Abby of someone. I'd like to bring up the name and see if it jogs her memory.'

Andrew sighed. Trust a woman to fixate on something that had nothing to do with the case. Then he remembered he was concerned for a woman—a very special woman.

And if Abby could help...

Jess heard the car drive away and knew the time had come. She looked at Rowan and saw kindness in his face.

'I'm Mrs Cochrane's granddaughter,' she said. 'My mother told me nothing about herself—her past, her family—apart from the fact that she'd had to leave her home. I didn't know a thing about her until she died and I found her birth certificate, a bus ticket from Riverview to Sydney which, I assume, dated from when she left town and some other legal papers where she'd changed her name from Cochrane to Chapman not long before I was born.'

'You have these papers?'

Jess shook her head.

'They're with the photo, in the frame, behind the print. I wanted to keep them somewhere safe.'

Her lips trembled on the words as the loss of that picture struck deep into her heart, but she pulled herself together and swallowed hard.

'Did Mrs Cochrane know?'

Jess shook her head.

'The birth certificate gave Riverview, the hospital, as Mum's place of birth. I didn't know if there'd be any Cochranes still here, although I guessed there'd be people who had known my mother. Mrs Cochrane being in the annexe was a coincidence.'

She paused, then admitted, 'When I arrived here and discovered who she was, I actually took it as a sign that I was doing the right thing.'

'Why didn't you tell her?'

How to explain?

'I knew nothing of what had happened—why my mother had cut herself off from her family.' She looked at Rowan, wondering if he'd understand her doubts and uncertainty. 'I thought Mrs Cochrane might not want to know I was her granddaughter. That my mother might have hurt her at some time...' She stalled, but knew, having come this far, she had to tell the rest.

'I thought I might have been the cause of the problem. There was no wedding certificate—just the change of name

by deed poll. The date on the bus ticket suggested my
mother was already pregnant when she left town.'

'But that would hardly be your fault,' Rowan pointed
out, and Jess felt fleeting gratitude for this support.

'No, but an older person might not have thought that
way, so I waited. I decided to get to know her better, let
her get to know me, and I hoped she'd eventually talk to
me—tell me about my mother, about what had happened.'

'And did she?' he asked. 'Is that what made you cry?'

Jess nodded.

'She didn't say much,' she explained. 'Just that it was
her fault she'd lost her daughter—that she'd sent her away!'

'Jessica!' Rowan's voice was so stern she was startled
out of her memory of the old woman's voice.

'Yes?'

He sighed and shook his head.

'Damn it all, don't you see? Andrew's right. You *should*
have a solicitor. We've already established you had the
opportunity to kill her, as you've no one to give you an
alibi. The means were there and now you're admitting she
upset you, that she told you of her cruelty to your mother.
All we need is to find she's left you all her money in her
will, and you'll have three motives.'

'But I needed her alive,' Jess told him, staggered by
these conclusions. 'Don't you understand? More than ever,
I needed her alive. I had to ask her something. *Had* to,
Rowan, had to know!'

'And if you asked, and she gave the wrong answer, what
then?'

She looked at him in horror.

'No! It wasn't that kind of question. It was personal.
Something only she would know—well, she and one other
person. But it wasn't dangerous, not even very important
at that stage.' She felt the weight of her assumptions press
against her heart. 'Well, not to anyone but me,' she added.

'What was it?' he asked. 'Tell me and let me judge for myself.'

She nodded, aware he was right, then realised, not knowing all the ramifications, he'd think she was overdramatising it.

'I wanted her to tell me who my father was.'

She stared across the cabin, seeing the bedroom through the open door, the bedside table where she'd kept her precious photograph.

'That's why I came here originally. To find whatever bits of family I might have left. I didn't intend to stage a great dramatic reunion, but I knew my mother had loved him— she'd told me that much when I'd asked about him—and I wanted to know, for my own sake.'

She shrugged because if it sounded weak in her ears, how much worse would it sound to Rowan?

'I didn't plan past finding out. I guess I thought whatever happened would happen after that. Then…'

'Then?'

He prompted her again, and when she didn't answer he guessed.

'You've been here three weeks, spent a deal of time with her—yet you hadn't asked. She was an old lady. She could have died any time, but you didn't ask this thing you say you had to know.'

'I didn't know I had to know it,' Jess told him, and she dropped her head into her hands to hide her fears. 'Not so urgently!'

Noises outside suggested that Sarah and Andrew had returned. She looked up towards the door and waited, half fearful, half resigned, to read their lack of success in Sarah's face as she preceded Andrew through the door.

'I'll take these to the station,' Rowan said, collecting the bag of roses off the table. He looked at Jess. 'You shouldn't be staying out here on your own, and I don't want you

leaving town. You could get a room at the motel, go back
to Andrew's—'

'Or come and stay in my spare bedroom,' Sarah said.
'Handy for work, and I promise I'll stop picking roses for
the duration of your visit.'

Jess felt the woman's kindness wrap itself around her
like a warm shawl.

'I'd like that,' she said, and tried to ignore the angry
light in Andrew's eyes.

Rowan shook hands with Andrew, nodded at Sarah, then
turned to Jess.

'I'll keep in touch,' he said, 'but, in the meantime, talk
to Andrew about that suggestion of his. He'll help you out
with this.'

Jess knew the policeman was being kind—he couldn't
know Andrew was the last person she should be leaning
on.

'And what was that cryptic remark supposed to mean?'
Andrew demanded, picking up handfuls of her clothes and
shoving them back into the case.

'He thinks I need a solicitor,' Jess told him, and heard
the sharp intake of air as Sarah gasped.

'Why?' the older woman asked, easing Andrew out of
the way and refolding the jumble of clothes and linen.

Truth time?

Jess knew it was, but still she hesitated.

In this case, the truth could hurt—not her, but Andrew
and his family.

'Because I make the perfect suspect,' she said lightly. 'I
was there, she'd made me cry, I'm a stranger in town—'

'Hell's bells, Jess, don't joke about this!' Andrew
growled. 'It's murder.'

She looked into his eyes and what she saw her tore her
apart.

'Do you think I don't know that?' she said sadly.

Then she turned away, crossing to the bathroom where she collected her toiletries and two wet uniforms.

'Let's get out of here,' she said to Sarah, and, taking care not to brush against the man she loved, she walked out of the cabin.

CHAPTER TEN

'HE'LL come after us, you know,' Sarah said. 'Andrew's not the kind of man to let you push him out of your life without some kind of explanation.'

'I can't explain to him,' Jess told her, and knew the flatness of her voice made the statement more emphatic than screaming it would have done.

'Why not?'

She glanced at Sarah who had her eyes on the road but all her attention, Jess knew, was attuned to her, and her reply.

Suddenly the need to talk to someone, anyone, about her dilemma overwhelmed her.

'It can't go any further, Sarah,' she said softly. 'It could be so destructive if it did.'

Sarah glanced her way, then back to the road, carefully turning onto the road for the short drive to the hospital grounds.

'I know about destructive forces, Jess, particularly in a small town. It won't go any further.'

Jess sighed. Now the time had come to tell it all, she wasn't sure where to begin.

'Start with Andrew,' Sarah suggested, as if she'd heard her thoughts.

'I think we might be half-siblings,' Jess whispered. 'And now she's dead I might never know. I can't take the risk that we are, and keep on seeing him. Can't explain my fears to him and start him wondering about his father. Do you understand the hurt it could spread in his family—the pain it could cause his mother, and his sisters? Andrew himself?'

'Whoa, there, Jessica!' Sarah said, stopping the car outside her flat and holding up her hand to stop the flow. 'I realise what you're getting at but what if you're not? What about that? Are you going to toss all you and Andrew had between you because of a possibility?'

'How can I not, if that possibility exists?' Jess demanded.

Sarah didn't answer, simply continued to sit in the car, staring straight ahead towards the annexe.

'OK,' she said, after a silence so long Jess had begun to wonder if Sarah could, like some other doctors she'd known, sleep upright. 'I understand what you're saying and I think I've got the broad picture here. You've never known who your father is, but knew or learned that your mother came from Riverview.'

She glanced at Jess, who nodded.

'Mrs Cochrane came into it?'

'She was my grandmother.'

'Oh, Jess, I'm so sorry. Dying like that, and so soon after your mother. No wonder you didn't want her cut.'

She gathered Jess into her arms, her warmth and sympathy so tangible that Jess allowed her grief for the old lady to steal over her, and she wept into Sarah's shoulder.

'There, isn't that better?' Sarah said briskly a little later. She handed Jess a handkerchief as she straightened up and sniffled miserably. 'And all this dreadful fear is because you didn't get around to asking her who fathered you? Is that it?'

Jess nodded.

'Did you tell Rowan this?'

'About being her granddaughter, yes, but not the rest. I don't know anything for sure and it didn't seem fair.'

'Being involved in a pregnancy and not taking responsibility for it isn't fair either,' Sarah reminded her. 'But I can see why you wanted to keep quiet—for Andrew's sake.'

She stared out through the windscreen again and Jess had the impression of a powerful intelligence at work.

'Of course, knowing you're the granddaughter would naturally make you Rowan's number one suspect. However, if he knew you needed her alive—'

'I told him that, but couldn't tell him why.'

Sarah groaned and rested her head in her hands for a moment.

'I can see your point. It's not particularly rational but, yes, I'd probably do the same. So let's look at this another way. What made you think it might be Andrew's father?'

Jess explained, beginning with Mrs Cochrane's admission that her daughter's lover had been married, then Andrew's conversation about the family leaving town before his birthday party.

'It does fit,' Sarah said slowly, 'but fitting doesn't always mean it's right.' She touched Jess lightly on the shoulder. 'I think you did very well, getting out of that restaurant. If it had been me, I'd have gone into strong hysterics on the spot and have had to be put away in a quiet rest home with softly padded walls for an indefinite period of time.'

Jess smiled at the picture Sarah's words conjured in her mind.

'And now I've got you smiling, let's adjourn to the flat. We'll eat, then think this through. There has to be a way to find out without involving other people.'

'Like asking Andrew's father, who'll then, should it not be true, be horrified that someone who could think such a thing might end up being his daughter-in-law?' Jess suggested dryly, following Sarah into the flat and dumping her suitcase on the floor inside the door. 'Great cornerstone for a relationship that would be!'

'No, we won't ask Andrew's father—well, at least not yet. Oh, why isn't Abby here? She knows everyone in town. In fact, her parents would have known your mother. Perhaps that's the way to go. Find friends of your mother's here in town and talk to them. Surely someone must have known who she was seeing.'

Sarah had continued on into the kitchen and was now peering into the refrigerator as if it might reveal ideas for the next stage of their investigation.

'Finding people who knew her is a good idea,' Jess said slowly, thinking through what Sarah had said. 'But how? Take out an ad?'

Sarah pulled a couple of packages out of the freezer and chuckled.

'I may not have been in this town long, but it has all the usual networks of any small town when it comes to who knows whom. And after going through the drama of Caroline Cordell's death recently, I even know some of the links. Carmel, Iain's receptionist in town, went to school with Abby. Your mother would be a lot older, but I bet Carmel knows someone who knows someone else.'

'But if it *was* Andrew's father, and his family left town to avoid a scandal, won't raising the subject now stir up talk that could still bounce back on him?'

'You're right, but you either want to know or you don't.'

'I could leave town, not knowing,' Jess said. 'If Rowan doesn't mention I was Mrs Cochrane's granddaughter, then there shouldn't be any talk.'

'Oh, there'll be talk. Especially if you're arrested for her murder. The potatoes are in the bottom of that cupboard. Get out two and start peeling them. We'll have chicken breasts and mashed potatoes and peas—real comfort food.'

Jess chuckled. 'I'm glad you've sorted out the priorities,' she said, feeling better than she had for two days. 'Peel the spuds before you go to jail.'

They worked together, then, as the meal cooked, Jess carried her suitcase into the spare bedroom and unpacked it.

'Why would someone take the photo of my mother?' she asked Sarah, when they'd eaten and, their stomachs content, were once again gnawing at the puzzle.

'I'm still stuck on proving paternity,' Sarah told her. 'Don't divert me onto other things.'

She began to scribble on a notepad.

'DNA is the easiest way, but we'd need blood or other cells from you—blood's easiest. Then we'd have to get some of your mother's—that's not so difficult if the facility where it was done has a decent policy about keeping samples. Then all we'd have to do is take blood from every male in town, aged between…how old was your mother?'

'You're not serious, are you?' Jess said, unable to believe Sarah was still scribbling.

'No, but sometimes when I write and talk things happen. You keep talking while I let my brain do its own thing for a few minutes.'

'If a DNA test could prove paternity, wouldn't siblings have similar DNA?'

'That's what I'm trying to work out. It would be easy to get some of Andrew's blood, but I think the parameters are too wide for us to do it easily or cheaply. Look!'

She waved Jess onto the couch beside her, and drew a series of strokes, some thick, some thin, some shaded, so the finished product resembled a bar code standing on its end.

'Say this is the child.' She pointed to the first line of strokes. 'Then if you check the two parents' DNA, they have to make up the child's exactly. See, we'll call this one Mum and this one Dad. In the same way as a child can get green eyes and blonde hair from one parent but a tendency to overweight from the other, so this child has these four lines of inherited material from Mum, the next line from Dad, another from Mum, then four from Dad, and so on.'

'Just like that?' Jess said, and Sarah grinned at her.

'Well, the bar codes are much bigger and more complicated, but believe me, kiddo, all the blips on your DNA must have come from either your mother or your father.'

'So if we lined up my DNA next to Andrew's?'

Sarah sighed.

'First we'd have to line yours up with your mother's and remove all the bits you inherited from her so we're left with your father's genetic input. Then we get Andrew's DNA tested, and his mother's—that should be fun—so we can take out what he got from her—'

'It's back to impossible again, isn't it?' Jess said, as the bubble of light-hearted fun burst.

'Or back to gossip. But maybe not with Carmel. I've had another brainwave. Andrew must know Abby's parents. They're more in the right age group for a bit of research, and if Abby's mother is even half as discreet as Abby she won't tell a soul we've been asking questions.'

She looked at Jess for confirmation that the idea was acceptable.

'It's better than doing nothing,' she agreed. 'Could we go tomorrow? Are you working? I'm sorry, Sarah, to be involving you in all of this.'

Sarah stood up and patted the top of her head.

'You've no idea how good it is to be able to help,' she said. 'I ran away from a similar situation once, Jess, and have always regretted it. Maybe fighting through this for you is my way of redeeming myself.'

She crossed to the phone, dialled a number and waited.

'He's not there,' she said, dropping the receiver back onto its cradle.

But Jess knew that already. She'd just heard Andrew's footsteps coming along the walkway from the hospital, and had seen his shadow as he'd passed the window.

He knocked in a perfunctory manner then walked in, a manila folder tucked under one arm.

'I'd have been here sooner but had a call to a road accident,' he said, more to Sarah than to Jess. 'Turned out old Freddie Klimp had tried to drive home from the pub. He ran his car into the school bus, which was parked and empty a hundred yards up the road. He got out to check the damage then felt tired, so he lay down on the footpath to have a sleep.'

'And someone called it in as an accident?' Sarah said, holding up the coffeepot and raising her eyebrows in a silent question.

'Love one,' Andrew replied, answering the unasked question first. 'And, of course, someone called it in. I mean, they could see the car all banged up against the bus, and there was the body lying right beside it.'

He sat down across from Jess, not touching her, just being there—and unsettling her unbearably.

'So,' he continued, when Sarah had brought coffee, mugs, milk and sugar and set them on the low table, 'where do we go from here? How do we find Jessica's stalker? Shall we give up on Kristie and take another tack?'

Jess stared at him, unable to believe this new Andrew. It was as if he'd taken her at her word, and had removed himself, mentally if not physically, from her orbit. Finding the stalker was now a bit of fun. A challenge.

'Well?' he said to her.

'Why are you doing this?' she asked.

'Because I don't like people frightening other people,' he said calmly. 'Don't worry, Jess, I've got the message. From now on all contact will be purely professional—apart from the sleuthing which you may or may not join in, depending on your own personal preferences.'

'But where do we start?' Sarah asked him.

'Here, at the hospital. With the employees.'

'Why? There'd be close to fifty if you include the support staff and those in the annexe.'

'Why? Because we have to begin somewhere. And I think we can narrow it down a bit. Let's consider who would have been here on Thursday morning and might have seen Jess come out of Mrs Cochrane's room.'

'We need the staff rosters for that,' Sarah told him.

'Which I have!' he said triumphantly, dropping the manila folder on the table and opening it.

Not that it told them much, Jess realised when they'd all
perused the papers and gloom had replaced optimism.
There had been two aides on duty in the annexe, but at that
time of the morning, when the residents had been getting
out of bed, it was unlikely either of them would have been
outside the building.

'The same applies to nursing staff and aides or orderlies
on the wards,' Andrew muttered, his enthusiasm visibly
dimmed by the dynamics of early morning routine. 'Although any one of them could have walked across the back
verandah to the washrooms at the time.'

'So we list them anyway, and what do we ask?' Sarah
said. 'Do we come right out and say, Did you see Jessica
crying on Thursday morning?'

'Oh, don't be stupid, Sarah!' Andrew scowled at her. 'As
if the guilty person would admit seeing her.'

He'd thought this would be easy. In his mind it had been
a sensible, logical approach. He'd also told himself he
could cope with Jessica's rejection, although in his heart he
knew he *had* to sort this out for his sake as well as hers.

What he hadn't counted on was his body turning his
brain to dog-food the moment he was close to her.

'Then what do you suggest, oh, great and mighty mind?'
Sarah asked.

He threw another scowl her way.

'What about the garden staff?' Jess asked. 'What time
do they start work?'

Andrew shuffled through the papers he'd filched off
Helen's desk.

'She doesn't seem to have them listed. Well, why would
she? There's the older fellow, Stan, who spends all his time
at work driving the ride-on mower over the grass, and the
young kid, whose name escapes me. They probably come
to work whenever they feel like it.'

'His name's Joe,' Jess told him. 'I met him in the kitchen on Thursday morning. He's got a beautiful smile.'

'Joe's the best!' Sarah said.

'Do you know him *that* well?' Andrew asked. 'I mean, he hasn't been here all that long, has he?'

Sarah chuckled.

'It's what he says if you're kind to him. ''You're the best, Doctor,'' he'll say if I stop for a chat.'

'Well, he told me Mrs Astbury was the best when I met him,' Jess teased her, then the smile slid from her face as she swung back to look at Andrew. 'You say he hasn't been here long? Would Rowan have considered him when he looked into strangers in the town?'

'Oh, Joe's not a stranger. He was here well before you arrived.' Sarah answered for Andrew. 'He was here when I came, which is roughly two months ago, and from the way Abby spoke he was a fixture then.'

She turned to Andrew for confirmation.

He shook his head.

'I really can't remember when he came. I know he was here before I left, then I was away for six weeks with the conference then leave. I suppose that's why he still seems newish to me.'

'Well, if he's been here that long, he certainly didn't follow me here, did he?' Jess said.

'So we cross Joe off the suspect list?' Andrew asked

'I think so,' Sarah said. In a sudden conversation switch that startled Jess, she added, 'Do you know Abby's parents? Could you talk to her mother and ask if it's OK for Jess and me to visit them?'

Jess opened her mouth to protest but Sarah silenced her with a warning frown.

'Why Abby's parents?' Andrew demanded, as Jess had known he would.

Sarah smiled sweetly at him.

'I'm working on the case,' she assured him. 'I'm following the ''who is Kristie'' line of questioning. The fact that Jess reminded Abby of someone has always niggled at me. I thought I'd run her by Abby's mother to see if she notices any resemblance to anyone.'

Jess hoped her relief wasn't too obvious. On its own the idea had a lot of merit, and if they could find out who had known her mother at the same time...

Hope began to banish the darkness of despair and she smiled at the woman who was being so kind to her.

'Great idea. I'll come with you,' Andrew announced, sending hope reeling back to its corner.

'You can't, you're on call,' Sarah reminded him with unflattering promptness. 'Jess and I are quite capable of handling a simple identity enquiry on our own.'

She winked at Jess, who responded with a weak smile. She was being pummelled by so many conflicting emotions that she couldn't find the exercise much fun.

'Then I'll come up and do a round and talk to any staff on our list who happen to be at work tomorrow morning,' Andrew declared. 'Not obviously, just chat about routines.'

He'd finished his coffee and knew he should leave, but couldn't bring himself to get up and walk away. Instinct suggested that these two women knew things they weren't telling him, but how to get it out of them?

'Have you checked on Giles Cameron this evening?' he asked Sarah, hoping he might be able to separate the pair.

'He's your patient, and you're here, so check on him yourself,' she said briskly. 'I'm too old to fall for that divide and conquer stuff.'

He grinned at her, then turned to Jess.

'And I don't suppose I could persuade you to walk back to the hospital with me? Perhaps take a turn around the verandah?'

She shook her head, and as the arc of dark hair swung heavily around her face he felt her sadness and inner despair and knew he shouldn't have asked, no matter how much he wanted to be with her.

'Then I'll be off,' he said.

'Phone Abby's mother from here before you go,' Sarah reminded him. 'Ask if it's OK, and what time would suit her.'

Pleased to delay his departure, he made the call and an appointment for ten o'clock, but his mind was puzzling over what was going on, tracking back through all he knew as he searched for something he might have missed.

'I'll be off, then,' he said, lingering between the kitchen bench, where the phone was, and the door.

Neither of the women argued with this suggestion. In fact, they were holding themselves still, as if immobilised by his presence. Just waiting to continue their plotting as soon as he left the room.

He muttered goodnight, and obliged, frustrated by his own inadequacy in solving the mystery and setting Jessica's life back on the right track.

'He's not happy about any of this,' Sarah said, when the door finally closed behind him.

Jess nodded, upset because she knew she'd caused his pain.

'But wasn't that a brilliant idea of mine about the resemblance thing and Abby's mother?' Sarah added.

This time Jess responded more appropriately, smiling at her friend as she confirmed, 'Brilliant!'

But her heart wasn't in the praise and Sarah must have heard the sorrow in her voice.

'Go to bed,' she said firmly. 'There's nothing more we can do tonight, and who knows what tomorrow might bring?'

Tomorrow brought Rowan—in uniform this time, so Jess felt a clutch of fear tighten her intestines as she opened the door to his knock.

'I've spoken to Mrs Cochrane's solicitor and he'd like to see you. He's agreed to go into his office for an hour or so, although it's Sunday. Apparently he has some other appointment as well. Are you available now?'

Jess turned back towards Sarah who was working her way through her second wake-up cup of coffee.

'We don't have to be at Mrs Franklin's until ten so go with the man. Get out of here. Waking up to someone with such caged energy is too much for an aging woman like me!'

Jess smiled at the complaint, then explained to Rowan, 'I don't have transport.'

'I'll take you,' he said easily. 'I've a visiting dignitary due at ten myself, so could Sarah pick you up after we've seen the solicitor? It's Hammond and Hammond, in the old stone building in the main street.'

Sarah nodded.

'I'll be there at a quarter to ten, which will give us time to drive out to the Franklins'. Off you go.'

She waved Jess away and, unable to think of a reason for not going, Jess obeyed.

'I've left my car in the car park—didn't know if you were working or not,' Rowan said. 'If we cut across the grounds it's quicker.'

She nodded her agreement and he took her arm to steady her as she stepped off the walkway.

'What does he want, the solicitor?' she asked, feeling more at ease with Rowan—perhaps because of the light clasp he'd retained on her elbow.

'It's about the will.'

She'd already guessed that and his voice told her nothing more.

'Good or bad?' she asked lightly.

He shrugged.

'That I don't know. The man's being deliberately obstructive at the moment. I told him who you were, thinking that might help. I don't suppose you've found the photograph and those papers.'

Jess shook her head.

They'd reached the big four-wheel-drive vehicle favoured by the police in the country areas, and Rowan opened the door for her, then passed her the seat belt, before closing it and walking around the bonnet to take his place behind the wheel.

'I suppose he might have questions for you about your mother. Perhaps he hopes to discover if you really are Mrs Cochrane's granddaughter.'

'But I can get copies of the certificates as proof, and so could he. It's a simple matter of applying to the registry office and paying some money.'

'He knows that, and in case he didn't I've already reminded him,' Rowan told her, as he drove steadily back to town.

'Well, at least it's something different to worry about,' Jess said resignedly. 'An obstructive solicitor!'

He pulled up outside the two-storey building Jess guessed had been built at the same time as Andrew's lovely cottage.

'The solicitor is Neville Hammond. The family has looked after the town's affairs for generations. His father dealt with the old lady first, but his father's now retired and, like everyone else in this case, uncontactable.'

He ushered Jess through the front door and up an impressive cedar staircase.

'Neville? You here somewhere?' he called when he reached the top.

A youngish man appeared, looking flustered rather than welcoming.

'Miss Chapman, is it? I'm sorry to drag you down here, but if I could just get some details. My father—Cam—'

'Let's sit down somewhere,' Rowan suggested. 'Your office?'

The other man pulled himself together with a visible effort, but his manner made Jess wonder if he wouldn't rather have studied anything but law. No doubt the family tradition made another choice impossible, but he didn't engender a lot of confidence in her.

She followed the two men into a large, sunny office and sank obediently into a soft leather chair.

'My problem is that Mrs Cochrane's will specifically appointed Cam Cordell as executor, but apparently the old lady never got around to telling Cam this and he's not at all happy about it.'

Neville Hammond looked as if he might burst into tears, making Jess wonder about this Cam Cordell's power in town.

'In fact, he's refusing to honour the commitment. He flew right off the handle when I told him what she'd asked him to do. Said he won't do it and that's that. So I thought…' he looked hopefully at Jess '…if I could establish the beneficiary without him it would be easier all round, but I need someone's permission to give details to the police and I don't have anyone, with Cam refusing to do his duty—'

'What does he have to do, as executor?' Rowan asked. 'Aside from giving permission for me to see the document which I can do anyway through a search warrant.'

Jess was surprised by the shift in his manner, from kind and helpful to gruff and businesslike, but apparently it worked for Mr Hammond. His hands stopped fluttering over papers spread like confetti on his desk and settled, clasped together, in front of him.

'He's been charged to find Mrs Cochrane's daughter and the child she was expecting at the time she left home, and bring her back to Riverview to claim her inheritance.'

Jess felt sadness that her mother hadn't lived to hear those words vie with an urge to smile because she guessed Mr Hammond had just told Rowan all he needed to know.

Or not quite?

'Does all the estate go to the daughter? Is there a provision to pay Cam for his search? Has anything been left to him?' Rowan asked.

The lawyer ticked off the questions on his fingers.

'Yes, it goes to the daughter and no to the others. Cam gets nothing but a load of work he doesn't need.' He glanced apologetically at Jess. 'They're his words not mine, but he was really upset when I told him. Shattered, in a way. Then, when he'd calmed down a bit, he said they'd been at odds for so long, he and the old lady, that the only possible reason she could have named him executor was to annoy him from the grave. To haunt him, he said.'

'Why would she have done it?' Jess asked, refusing to believe the frail old woman she'd known, though briefly, could have been so vindictive.

'Probably for that very reason,' Rowan told her. 'She's fought with everyone in town over the years, but she always kept her best battles for Cam. She led the fight to stop the council from developing the land along the river into a kind of entertainment park—restaurants, tourist shops, kiddie rides, that kind of thing. She pointed out that most of Riverview's tourists came to get away from that kind of thing, while he and his mates on the council felt it would attract tourists.'

'And who was right?' Jess asked, distracted by this glimpse of her grandmother's spirit.

'Oh, she was, but Cam was the only person in town, apart from her, of course, with the money to build the place. He took his defeat personally.'

'He'd bought up land adjacent to the river then lost a lot of money with the setback, so I guess he was bitter,' Neville Hammond added, sounding almost pleased at Cam's defeat.

Apart from the fact that his daughter had been killed not long before Jess had arrived in Riverview, she didn't know much about the man. And the more she heard of him, the less desire she had to change that status.

'So, getting off Cam Cordell, where do we stand now?' Rowan asked.

The lawyer looked at Jess.

'Rowan tells me you've lost the papers, but that's OK. I have your mother's birth date, but I'd like yours as well.' Jess obliged. 'Now, have you any idea of when she changed her name?'

'It was the November before I was born, but I don't have the exact date.'

Mr Hammond beamed at her.

'Don't you worry about that,' he said. 'I'll take it from there and I'll check out the legalities of Cam's behaviour as well. I think it would be easiest if I can bypass him and deal directly with you.' He notched up his smile to an even higher brilliance. 'Providing, of course, you are who you say you are, and I have no doubt about that.'

'Some lawyer,' Rowan muttered, as they made their way down the stairs a little later. 'Leaping to conclusions with absolutely no proof whatsoever.'

Jess felt the fear creep over her again, but she fought it off, made it safely to the bottom of the steps, then turned to face him—to challenge him.

'You're not so willing to be taken in, though, are you, Rowan?'

He looked into her eyes.

'I go on facts, not feelings,' he said firmly. 'And right now the facts aren't looking too healthy for you.' Then he smiled and she saw how attractive he was. 'But, on the other hand, it doesn't feel right to me. None of it. There's something I've missed. Something so damned obvious I can't see it. But until I find it don't leave town, and make damn sure you're with someone all the time. No going off on your own, understand? No heroics.'

Jess was so overwhelmed by his concern that she stretched up and kissed him on the cheek.

'Thank you for saying that,' she said softly, drawing back as she realised the front door had swung open and someone had walked in. Someone she'd just as soon not have seen, and from the look on Andrew's face he'd just as soon not have seen that grateful kiss.

'Jessica. Rowan.'

He nodded twice then took the steps two at a time, calling to Neville Hammond as he went, leaving Jess with such utter sadness in her heart that she forgot the fear.

CHAPTER ELEVEN

THE Franklins' farm was a short drive from town and, according to Andrew's directions, fairly easy to find.

Sarah listened quietly as Jess explained what had happened in the solicitor's office.

'I've only met him a couple of times,' she told Jess in answer to a question about Cam Cordell. 'I wasn't particularly impressed, but as his daughter had just been killed I cut him a bit of slack. He was genuinely devastated by her death.'

Jess asked what had happened, and the explanations took them to their destination.

Sarah parked under a shady pepper tree, and as they approached the house they saw a woman appear on the wide verandah.

'Sarah and Jessica, I presume,' she said, coming down the steps to greet them.

Sarah gave her name and offered her hand, then introduced Jess.

'Well, come on in,' Mrs Franklin said. 'I've made tea and I've some scones and Anzac biscuits fresh from the oven.'

She turned to lead the way into the house, then swung back to look at Jessica again. Sarah, wondering how she was going to raise the question of the nurse's paternity, thought nothing of it until they were seated, tea poured and the scones passed around.

Then Mrs Franklin said, 'Look, I know you've come to talk about something else entirely, some trouble at the hospital, but when you turn your head a certain way, Jessica, you look so like someone I knew.'

'Virginia Cochrane?' Jess said eagerly.

Sarah saw the hope die from Jess's eyes as Mrs Franklin looked startled and said, 'Why Virginia? For goodness' sake, I haven't thought about her for years! No, my dear, it was Abby's friend Caroline you reminded me of. When she was young, of course. A teenager. Before she went all glamorous. I don't suppose you're related to the Cordells?'

Jess looked bewildered and shook her head, but Sarah's neurones were synapsing at such speed she could hardly keep up with them.

'I think you've probably answered what we came to ask you,' she said to Mrs Franklin. 'But, please, can what we say remain in confidence between us?'

Abby's mother stared at her for a moment, then said, 'I'm not a gossip and, yes, whatever you say won't go beyond this room.'

Sarah smiled to think her guess about this woman had been correct.

'We came to ask what you knew of Mrs Cochrane's daughter. We thought you might have known her when she was young—before she went away.'

Sarah glanced at Jess, who seemed to have recovered somewhat, although Sarah doubted whether she'd made the connection.

'I'm Virginia Cochrane's daughter,' Jess said. 'That's why I thought—although I always knew I didn't take after my mother.'

Sarah watched as Mrs Franklin reassessed her visitor and blinked away a tear.

'She was older than me, Ginny, but such fun! So friendly. Even to those of us who weren't particularly close to her. Perhaps it was because she didn't put on airs the way her mother did. There was no "Lady of the Manor" nonsense about Ginny.'

Mrs Franklin hesitated, then, perhaps sensing the tension in the room, said, 'But she's still alive, surely.'

'She died suddenly not long ago,' Sarah explained, to save Jess the strain of talking about it.

'She never talked about the past, never married,' Jess explained, 'but when she died and I found she'd been born here I had to come, to find out something about her life.'

Mrs Franklin leaned forward and took Jess's hand.

'Of course you did. I didn't know she'd had a child! There was talk, of course, when she left town, but I don't remember anyone ever suggesting she might be pregnant. Not Ginny. We all just assumed she'd argued with her mother. The old lady was a dreadful tartar.'

She blew her nose, then collected herself.

'And have you found out what you needed to know? Oh, dear, didn't someone tell me Mrs Cochrane had died? Poor child.'

She patted Jess again and Sarah began to wonder if they'd ever get any further than the wonder and sympathy. The scones and biscuits were delicious, but she and Jess were here for a purpose.

Jess must have felt the same way for it was she, apparently oblivious to the resemblance connection, who steered the conversation back on track.

'I want to find out who my father is,' she said firmly. 'As far as I can gather, my mother became pregnant and her mother immediately refused to have anything more to do with her. Do you know anyone she might have told? All I know is that the man was married. Mrs Cochrane, my grandmother, told me that much.'

Mrs Franklin looked at Jess again, and lifted her hand to press it against her chest.

'Oh, dear, let me think. It can't be right. He's the very last person I'd have thought. Although...'

'Who?' Jess asked, leaning forward in her chair, her hands trembling as if she wanted to rip the answer from Mrs Franklin's throat.

'Why, Cam, of course. He was still married to Caroline's

mother at the time, but now I come to think about it they
did break up not long after Ginny left town. Perhaps his
wife knew he'd had an affair. That might explain the split.
He married again, of course, before Christine, his present
wife. She's his third.'

'That's why Mrs Cochrane did it? Appointed him, of all
people, to look for us?' Jess looked to Sarah. 'You
guessed?'

'When Mrs Franklin mentioned the resemblance, I wondered. Now, of course, we *could* do a DNA test, if he
agreed.'

Sarah saw a shudder rip through Jess's body.

'I don't know that I want him for a father,' she said. 'A
man like that!'

'Perhaps later,' Sarah suggested, knowing Jess was still
shocked by the revelation and not in any condition to be
making decisions. 'But what of Andrew's family?'

She turned to Mrs Franklin. 'Did you know them? The
Kendalls. He was a teacher here—left town about the same
time.'

'Alistair Kendall? A lovely man. In fact, it was a funny
thing. He and Cam Cordell were best friends from when
they started school. Vague relations, I think, as well, although I know Andrew doesn't have much to do with the
family. Anyway, one day they had this dreadful argument
in the centre of town, and the next thing we knew the
Kendalls were gone.'

'Maybe I do need the DNA test,' Jess whispered.

'To tell if you're Cam Cordell's child?' Mrs Franklin
asked. 'Don't bother. Wait a minute—I'll find some photos.'

She bustled off and came back with an album, opening
it on the table and leafing through it.

'Ah, I knew I had one. Abby and Caroline in their school
uniforms the year they went to boarding school. They were
just sixteen, the pair of them. See.'

She pointed to the dark-haired girl and Sarah saw the resemblance, but many dark haired people must look alike.

Jess nodded at it, then said, 'It couldn't have been the other way around? Not this Alistair Kendall—'

'Alistair Kendall your father? No way! He worshipped his wife.' Mrs Franklin stared into the distance, as if seeing back to those days. 'It seems so long ago. She was lovely, Rowena, such a nice-natured young woman. Always helping out anyone in trouble. In fact, I often thought that if Ginny had kept in touch with anyone it would have been her.'

Jess knew she should have been reassured but her uneasiness persisted.

Not that she could blame Mrs Franklin.

'Thank you for being so helpful,' she said, glancing across to Sarah to check it was OK for them to leave.

Sarah responded by rising to her feet.

'You've been most kind,' she said to Mrs Franklin. 'Perhaps we'll meet again before Abby and Iain get back and I'm off somewhere else.'

'Come any time,' their hostess said, then she leaned over and kissed Jess on the cheek. 'And Ginny's daughter will always be welcome in my house. Take care, my dear, and do come again.'

'Well, how has all that left you feeling?' Sarah asked when they were back on the main road to town.

'More confused than ever?' Jess suggested, and Sarah chuckled.

'Would it be so bad to be Cam's daughter? Surely you should be happy he's shifted into the front running ahead of Andrew's dad.'

'But no one likes him! What could my mother have seen in him! Even now, look at his behaviour in not wanting to look for my mother. Doesn't that show a total disregard for tackling his responsibilities?'

'He may have his reasons, Jess,' Sarah said gently. 'Don't judge him yet.'

'Well, when can I judge him? After I've been to see him and demanded to know the truth?'

She might have sounded brave about it, but she dreaded the thought of tackling the man who'd been so callous.

Sarah didn't answer for a few minutes, but as they drove through the town to turn towards the hospital she said, 'That might not be a bad idea, but let's sit down first and put together all we know. I think we should consider any possible consequences before you go rushing into battle with Riverview's most powerful man.'

Andrew's car was parked in the hospital car park and Andrew himself was parked in Sarah's living room.

Jess's body went into its rejoicing routine with heart acceleration, lung constriction and a knotting of her intestines. Suddenly, facing up to Cam Cordell seemed a very good idea!

Once she knew…

'I'm handier here if the hospital needs me,' Andrew was saying, by way of apology to Sarah. 'And you should lock up. Anyone could walk in here.'

He nodded at Jess.

'I went to see Neville Hammond to ask him to represent you—but apparently he already does.'

Jess frowned, her internal excitement dampened by his repressive tone.

Surely the solicitor couldn't have told him—

'Enough of sidetracks,' Sarah told him. 'Forget the solicitor. What have you learned? Do you have any news? Did you find out anything?'

She dropped onto the lounge and waved Jess to sit beside her.

'Only that half the hospital uses the back verandah to sneak an illicit cigarette, but no one ever sees anything. Not even the person poisoning their lungs beside them. It's a conspiracy of silence—or should that be of sight?'

'And no luck with Kristie?' Sarah persisted, then she straightened up and stared at Andrew. 'What were you saying last night about a soap star?'

'She's the only Kristie I can come up with,' he said, his voice flat with defeat. 'Apparently there's a show on TV about all these nubile young women who share a flat, and Cam's daughter used to play the part of one of them. Her character was called Kristie.'

Jess and Sarah turned and looked blankly at each other.

'S-surely it c-can't be that easy!' Jess stuttered.

'We need a tape of the show or a picture of her in the part,' Sarah said.

'What on earth are you two talking about?' Andrew demanded.

Jess felt a smile trembling on her lips as she looked at him. She was both excited and relieved that finally they might be making some sense of the mystery.

And very tentatively hopeful that the outcome might be good.

'There's a lot you don't know and we'll explain it all later, but Mrs Franklin thinks Jess might be Cam Cordell's child, so if someone was attracted to Caroline as Kristie, he—or perhaps she—might have mistaken Jess for this Kristie person.'

'I don't understand a word you're saying and I have absolutely no idea of where you'd get a video of the show.' He'd barely got the words out when he hit his forehead with the heel of his hand. 'Hey! Hold up a minute—maybe I do. Perhaps the Redmans might have one.'

'Who are the Redmans?' Jess and Sarah chorused the question.

'Come with me,' Andrew replied. 'Mrs R. and young Christopher are still here.'

He led the way over to the hospital and into the blue

maternity suite. The new mother was sitting up in bed, reading a magazine, baby Christopher asleep in a crib by the bed.

'Ah, visitors, how nice,' she greeted them.

'We've a strange request,' Sarah said, after the introductions had been completed. 'Would you by any chance have—at home, of course—any pictures or videos of the serial Caroline Cordell was in?'

'*18 Park Lane*?' Mrs Redman asked.

Jess held her breath as Sarah confirmed the name of the show.

'I've always been a fan of it, but I'm not one for collecting pictures,' the patient began. 'There might be an episode on video from some time when we were going out but I usually tape over things once I've seen them.'

She looked at the three faces and no doubt read their disappointment.

'What did you need to know?'

Jess looked at Andrew, who shrugged helplessly and turned to Sarah for help.

'We wondered about Kristie,' Sarah explained. 'I mean, did she look like Caroline looked in real life?'

Mrs Redman beamed at her.

'Oh, no! Caroline was getting on, you know. Older than me. But the show's about these young people, eighteen or so. Kristie in the show was much younger than Caroline really was and she wore her hair straight with a fringe in front. It must have been a wig because Caroline's hair was quite wavy and she had streaks in it when she came home.'

She nodded towards Jess.

'In fact, she looked more like you do, Kristie on the show did, with that dark straight hair. Like Caroline as a teenager, my Mum says. I've seen you around the hospital, of course, but you usually wear your hair pulled back so I didn't notice the resemblance before.'

Jess felt her chest constrict, and from the stillness of her two companions she knew they were feeling the same way.

Sarah managed to thank Mrs Redman for her help and offer an excuse for them to be on their way. They walked out of the room, Jess grateful for Andrew's support as he slid his hand beneath her elbow and steadied her.

The rose was on the doormat outside Sarah's flat, and the note said simply, 'Kristie's the best.'

Birdsong filled the sudden silence as they stared in horror at the note. High trills of sound beating out the seconds.

'Joe!'

Andrew said the name that had ricocheted into Jess's head, the phrasing of the words familiar to them all.

He crushed the rose in his hands, seemingly oblivious to the pain of the thorns.

'I'll phone Rowan,' Sarah said.

'Is Joe at work today? Does he work weekends? Let's find him,' Andrew fumed. He turned as if to start a major search but Jess grasped his arm and held him back.

'It might not be him,' she warned. 'Sarah's right. We have to let the police handle it.'

'And I'm supposed to just sit here and wait?'

Jess smiled at his impatience then realised there was something else *she* needed to find out.

'No,' she said. 'You can drive me to Cam Cordell's place. I have to talk to him.'

He looked down into her face, his eyes full of tenderness and hope.

'Will this sort out what went wrong between us?' he asked.

'I hope so,' she said softly. 'Now, give the rose to Sarah, and let's go.'

Young Billy Cordell's babysitter directed them to the council chambers where an official welcome for a visiting politician was under way.

'Do we wait, or beard him among the dignitaries?' Andrew asked.

'Beard him—I've waited long enough,' Jess said, deciding it was time to take control.

The official part was over and guests had spilled out into the council gardens and were sipping tea and eating cakes.

'That's him over there,' Andrew told her, taking her arm and weaving a path through the small crowd.

'I'm not really dressed for this,' Jess whispered, as she realised her jeans and T-shirt made her stand out among the flowery dresses of the other women.

'Don't get cold feet at this stage,' Andrew said. 'Ah, here we are. Good morning, Cam. May I introduce Jessica Chapman?'

Jess looked at the man who might be her father, and felt such a storm of emotion she thought she might have collapsed again had it not been for Andrew's arm around her waist.

'Could I speak to you—away from these people?'

He frowned at her and inched slightly away, and she heard the words before she realised she was going to say them.

'I'm Ginny's daughter.'

The fluctuating colour of his face was enough to tell her Mrs Franklin had been right.

He went red, then white, then red again.

'I didn't know—never guessed. I would have taken care of her—of you. She said she had to go because she loved me. Said she'd blame herself for ever if she broke up my marriage. Damn self-sacrificing woman. My marriage was all but over anyway!'

He turned and walked away from them, his head bent and his shoulders shaking.

'Well, that went well,' Andrew said. 'Do I gather from all that that you're Mrs Cochrane's granddaughter? That your mother was her daughter? Cam Cordell your father?'

He sounded angry but Jess found she couldn't cope with any more emotion. She nodded and looked around for somewhere to sit down.

Andrew must have guessed because he walked her to a chair, held her arm as she sat down and squatted beside her.

'And where do I come into all this? Why the sudden retreat, Jess? Why the fear I saw in your eyes when you looked at me?'

She touched his cheek and wondered if she'd killed the precious bud of love which had been unfurling between them. She decided he had to know what she'd been thinking.

'I came here to find my father. Mrs Cochrane told me he was married, and only hours later you told me about your family leaving town—a personal problem. I added that to my resemblance to your sisters, your father's strong genes—'

'You thought we might be siblings? Oh, Jess, my darling heart, how could you have thought that and not said anything?'

He took her hands and looked up into her face.

'What could I do?' she asked. 'Can you imagine the trouble it could have unleashed within your family?'

'So you went away? A damn self-sacrificing woman, like your mother?'

'Only until I'd asked her,' she told him. 'Asked Mrs Cochrane. Then, if it had been so, yes, I'd have gone away. I didn't need a family that badly.'

He stood up and bent to kiss her on the cheek, then he pulled her to her feet and kissed her lips.

'That's why you went to see her that morning. But she was already dead.'

He whispered the words, looking down into her face with so much love it eased the pain of the memory.

'Did Mrs Franklin tell you it was Cam?'

'She suggested it, and told me your family had left town after a fight with him. She was going on resemblances, not knowledge, but I think his reaction to my words confirmed it, don't you?'

Andrew glanced over her shoulder.

'If you want to hear it in words, he's heading this way now, albeit slowly.'

Jess shivered.

'I'm not sure,' she said. 'I know I need to hear it, but I—'

'Don't want him for a father? That's a perfectly natural reaction. I wouldn't either. But you might have to give him a chance. You're going to be living in the same small town as him for a very long time.'

Jess forgot Cam Cordell and smiled into the face of her beloved.

'I am?' she teased.

'You bet your life you are!'

'Why?'

'Because I love you and want to marry you, just as soon as we possibly can.'

'No, Andrew,' she said gently, as a cloud passed over her shining happiness. 'We're forgetting something else. Not being your sister, that certainly makes things easier, but I could be arrested for my grandmother's murder any minute now. I can't marry you with that hanging over our heads.'

'Ah! I'd forgotten that minor inconvenience. But you do love me?'

She smiled at his insistence.

'I do love you!' she agreed, as Cam Cordell took his last step towards them.

'I need to speak to you,' he said, ignoring Andrew and focussing on Jess.

'Perhaps some other time,' Andrew told him, moving closer to the woman who'd just admitted her love for him.

'There's only one thing we need to know right now. Are you her father?'

He nodded, and his big frame trembled as if the movement was a dreadful strain.

'If you are Ginny's daughter, and old enough to have been conceived here, then, yes,' he whispered huskily.

'I am Ginny's daughter, and my mother was pregnant when she left town,' Jess responded, and Andrew felt a matching tremor in her body. He nodded to Cam, and eased Jess away, avoiding the crowds as he led her to the car.

'Satisfied?'

She sighed and snuggled closer.

'One day I'll have to talk to him. Hear what he has to say. But, yes, for now it's enough to know, I guess.'

Andrew kissed her, then opened the car door.

'No guessing,' he said firmly. 'Together we can tackle the world. Now, let's go back to the hospital and see if Rowan's tracked down Joe.'

'Joe!'

Jess murmured the name.

'I can believe he left the roses, but murdering Mrs Cochrane? That doesn't make sense.'

'Nothing people like that do makes sense to a so-called normal person, Jess,' Andrew told her, and he rested his hand on her shoulder and gave the fine bones a gentle squeeze. 'Keep in mind that, to us, stalking people doesn't make sense either.'

Sarah was standing in the doorway of the flat.

'You've a job coming in,' she said to Andrew. 'Another autopsy. Joe's dead.'

'Dead?' Jess echoed. 'But he can't be! Now we'll never know what happened.'

Sarah put an arm around her and led her into the flat.

'Rowan went from here to where Joe lived—in another cabin in the caravan park. Joe had killed himself. He left a note. Apparently he saw Rowan taking you to his car this morning and thought you'd been arrested for Mrs Cochrane's murder.'

'So he killed himself?' Jess said, and heard the unaccustomed shrillness in her voice. 'That's terrible.'

'He'd killed your grandmother, Jess,' Sarah reminded her. 'And he didn't want you to take the blame.'

'But he never harmed me. Just left roses. And he had such a sweet smile.'

She couldn't bring herself to believe it.

Andrew wrapped his arms around her and said, 'Think about it later.' She took the easy option and simply rested against his chest, content to let her mind go blank. Except for love—that was there—and relief that she could stand in Andrew's arms without fear.

The strident summons of the phone recalled her to the real world and she listened to Sarah's part of the conversation, which seemed mainly assent of some kind.

'Rowan's coming here,' she said. 'Apparently he found the picture of you and your mother in Joe's cabin, along with an extensive collection of Kristie posters. He's been in touch with Joe's family. According to his mother, he's been treated for obsessive behaviour but had seemed stable enough on medication. Six months ago he became obsessed by Kristie, so much so that when Caroline came up here for her holiday he found out and followed her. Then, of course, she died, and one can only assume he stayed on for lack of anything better to do.'

'Until Jess arrived,' Andrew said. 'And he was able to transfer his fixation to her.'

'Exactly!'

Jess shuddered, and felt Andrew's arms tighten protectively around her.

'You should be in bed, my girl,' he said to her. 'You've had an overdose of emotion today.'

'You go and tuck her in,' Sarah suggested. 'I'll go across to the hospital and wait for Rowan.'

EPILOGUE

'I DON'T know how I ever let you talk me into this,' Jess complained, as she carried a jug of iced water out of the house and set it on a table in the backyard of the cottage.

'The engagement or the party?' Andrew replied, turning from the back fence where he'd been peering suspiciously into the next yard.

'The party!' she replied, willing the heat she was feeling to stay out of her cheeks. Not that Andrew was fooled. He was grinning at her and she knew he knew what she was thinking.

'What a pity!' he said softly, walking towards her. 'I was going to remind you how I talked you into the engagement.'

She lost the battle with the heat, but hid her face against his neck as he folded her into his arms.

'Was I unfair? I know I went too far too fast, but I love you so much, Jess. I wanted all the world to know you belonged to me.'

'You could never be unfair,' she told him, raising her head so she could press kisses on his jaw, his ear lobe. 'I was frightened—more by what was happening between us than by the roses, really. I'd always held back from relationships—stayed aloof—except for that one disastrous time.'

'Probably because, whether consciously or not, of your mother's experience. She'd told you she loved your father, and she must have, to have opted to keep his child—you.'

His arms tightened their grip on her.

'It's natural you'd be wary, but, oh, Jess, what a gift of love she gave to me as well. What if she hadn't had that

179

disastrous affair? Hadn't left the clues that set you searching for some hints about your life? I wouldn't have met
you, fallen in love, found my mate for life—for ever.'

She found his lips and kissed him properly, allowing the
love she felt for him to wipe away both the tears and fears
of the past, and her apprehension about the future—even
the immediate future.

The party!

'Hey, we can't be doing this. People will be arriving any
minute.'

'People already have.' Rowena Kendall came out of the
kitchen, a plate of savoury nibbles in her hand. 'Louise and
Tim are here and, according to them, Sue and Dan are not
far behind.'

'Oh, good, I want to see Louise,' Andrew announced,
abandoning the woman to whom he'd just pledged undying
love and striding into the house.

'He's always been like that,' Rowena told Jess. 'If something's on his mind, he wants it sorted out immediately.'

'Tell me about it!' Jess groaned, and they both smiled.
Rowena and Alistair had arrived the previous evening, and
had welcomed Jess into their family so openly and with
such affection that Jess had forgotten how nervous she'd
been about the meeting.

'Did Alistair talk to Cam?' she asked, knowing her prospective father-in-law was hoping to end the long-standing
estrangement on this visit.

'Did he talk to Cam?' Rowena rolled her eyes. 'He left
here after breakfast and just phoned to say they'd be a little
late. As you can imagine, they had a lot to catch up on
after twenty-six years.'

Jess looked at Rowena.

'And what should I do?' she asked the older woman.

'About your father? I don't know, my dear. I was so
angry when I found out he'd been seeing your mother I
refused to have anything more to do with him. At first,

Alistair pointed out that Ginny was old enough to know what she was doing, but I couldn't see it that way. For me, marriage was for keeps and it was Cam who'd made the vows. And Ginny, for all her maturity in a lot of ways, was an innocent as far as men were concerned.'

'Was she happy, do you think?' Jess asked.

'Oh, Jess,' Rowena said, 'she was! She was radiant. She glowed the way you do when Andrew's in the room. I know everyone says you look like Cam's side of the family, but I can see Ginny in you as well. Anyway, that's how I guessed she'd finally met someone special. Then I asked her who it was, and she wouldn't tell me so I knew it had to be someone she shouldn't be seeing.'

'And Cam?' Jess prompted.

'Well, for a start, he should never have married Cheryl. She was a city girl and she hated the country. He thought she'd grow to like it, but people don't change that much. Of course, by the time he realised it wasn't going to happen they'd had Caroline, and he adored the baby so he stayed in a marriage that offered him nothing.'

'Couldn't he have changed—enough to make a move to the city?'

Rowena smiled at her.

'Of course, but it wouldn't have occurred to him. And he'd have hated it as much as Cheryl hated the country. Here, even then, he was on his way to becoming a big fish in his own small pond. In the city, he'd have been lost.'

'So must my mother have been when she first arrived,' Jess reminded her, and Rowena took her in her arms, as Andrew had done earlier, and gave her a hug.

'But your mother had more guts and courage than ten Cam Cordells,' she said. 'I was so upset when she just disappeared like that. Oh, I guessed she'd gone to escape an impossible situation, but I thought she could have told me she was going, kept in touch with me. I felt I could have helped her, lent her money, been there as a friend.'

She released Jess and stroked her cheek.

'Of course, now I know she was pregnant at the time I can understand why she cut herself off so completely. She knew how I felt about marriage. She'd agonised over the wrongness of her affair even while she'd been so happy with him. I suppose she'd guessed that if he'd known she was pregnant he'd have divorced Cheryl and married her, and Ginny would have hated to have had that on her conscience.'

Jess sighed.

'There's so much to know, to learn.' She remembered something else. 'You said *you* were angry with Cam. Why did Alistair fight with him?'

Rowena smiled and Jess, sensitive to coloured cheeks, saw the warmth flood into the older woman's face.

'Because I was so angry! I was so upset when Ginny left that I blamed Cam, who'd been older, more experienced, married and should have known better. I think Alistair had heard all this from me so often that when Cam met him in the street and accused me of helping Ginny leave town, Alistair, who really agreed with me but had stuck up for Cam because he was a friend, suddenly let fly with all the things I'd been saying.'

'That would have made for an interesting diversion in Riverview!'

'It was the talk of the town—and in some ways probably helped with Ginny's escape because it wasn't until *we'd* left town and things settled down that anyone would have realised she was gone.'

'Poor Mum!' Jess whispered.

'Was she?' Rowena asked. 'I can't imagine Ginny letting anything get her down for very long. She was so naturally happy, and so alive. I simply assumed she'd have gone ahead and made her new life as joyous as her old one had been.'

Jess thought about it, then nodded.

'We *were* always happy,' she admitted slowly. 'She had a lot of friends—people she'd met at work, neighbours... Yes, you're right. She never brooded on the past or talked about regrets—or not to me.'

'Well, remember that,' Rowena told her. 'Look, here's Lou. She's the middle one. I do hope this isn't too much for you, meeting so many family all at once.'

Jess reassured her she would cope, and stepped forward to be introduced to Andrew's sister.

It was a perfunctory introduction, then Jess was left with Rowena and Tim while Andrew dragged his sister towards the back fence.

'What on earth's he doing?' Rowena asked.

Jess shrugged. 'I have no idea. He's been hanging over the back fence most of the morning.'

He looked back towards her as she spoke and waved to her to join them, but Sarah had arrived, and a couple Jess guessed were Sue and Dan. She ignored her errant fiancé and went to greet them.

'Abby and Iain are here as well,' Sarah told her, giving her a warm hug. 'They've been waylaid by Andrew's dad in the front garden.'

More introductions were performed, a continuing job as other hospital staff arrived to share the happy occasion.

Andrew left the back fence to play host, but every now and then Jess would catch sight of him waving his arms towards either the cottage or the back fence.

'What's going on with you and Louise?' she asked when they came together for long enough to share a few words.

'I've had the most wonderful idea,' he told her, his excitement shining in his eyes. 'For extensions. Lou's an architect. I think I told you that. We can attach a long structure, like a small stone barn, to the back of the cottage and leave all the bottom area open, but have a kind of mezzanine floor up high along one side for smallish bedrooms and a bathroom.'

Jess stared at him and shook her head, unable to follow the conversation at all.

'You're worried about losing the garden,' he said, completely misinterpreting her frown. 'But that won't have to happen because the old house behind is for sale, and we buy that, pull the house down and use the plot for a garden and play area and possibly a—'

'I'm not worried about losing the garden,' Jess broke in, because she'd learned by now that she sometimes had to do that with Andrew. 'I'm wondering why we need more bedrooms.'

'For the kids!' he said, in the kind of voice that suggested she was dense not to have realised. 'The cottage is too cramped—the little bedrooms will be OK while they're babies. But if we build the barn, the big area downstairs can be adapted as they grow—you know, train sets on the floor when they're little, and later on a table tennis table, then, when they all leave home, I can have a billiard table in there.'

Jess looked into the eyes of the man she loved.

'We're not married yet and you've already got the children leaving home?'

He grinned at her.

'Too far too fast?'

'Just a little,' she said faintly.

Rowena rescued her.

'Cam's here. I'll stick with you if you like.'

Andrew watched his mother put her arm around Jess's shoulders and walk with her to greet the man who was her father. He felt love tugging at his heart, and a sickness in his stomach as he realised what she was going through.

His feelings for Jess, his sense of oneness with her, were so overwhelming, was it any wonder he got carried away?

Sarah joined him and smiled when she saw where he was looking.

'I think you'll be very happy,' she said quietly.

'I know we will,' he told her, then he turned towards her.

'And you, Sarah? Where next for you?'

Sarah's smile faded.

'Back to Windrush Sidings to do a four-week locum,' she said softly. 'It's where I did my first year in a country hospital. I was so young, so green, it's a wonder there are any inhabitants left alive to treat.'

'Are you looking forward to it?'

Sarah hesitated.

'Looking forward to laying a few ghosts,' she admitted. 'And to seeing old friends. I've remained in touch with a number of the families, and as there's some kind of "Back to—" celebration happening while I'm there, I'll get to see a lot of folk I used to know.'

Andrew kissed her on the cheek.

'I can only wish you happiness, and thank you again for helping me find mine,' he said, then, as Jess crossed the garden towards them, he added, 'It's there for you, too, Sarah, I can feel it.'

Jess smiled in response to the silent messages he sent her, but it was to Sarah she turned.

'Your daughter—Lucy—phoned. She'd rung the hospital first and they gave her this number, but the connection was awful and she said to give you a message.'

'Yes?' Sarah said impatiently.

Jess frowned, as if concentrating on getting the words right, then grinned at Sarah.

'She said to tell you she'd changed her mind and would meet you in Windrush Sidings after all.'

Sarah gave a whoop of joy and hugged Jess and then Andrew.

'Great! Now I'll go and talk to Abby and leave you two lovebirds alone.'

'See how happy she is,' Andrew said, tucking Jess close to his side and surveying the activity in his backyard with

a proprietorial pleasure. 'That's because she has a daughter
Now try to tell me I'm going too far too fast when I make
plans for our children. When they leave home, as well as
having the space for the billiard table we'll still have the
bedrooms out here in the barn part so they can come back
with their kids or send the grandchildren to stay.'

Grandchildren?

Jess turned and kissed him, because she'd learned that
was another way she could stop his flow of words.

And because she loved him more than words could
ever say.

MILLS & BOON®

Makes
any time
special

Enjoy a romantic novel from
Mills & Boon®

Presents...™   *Enchanted*™   TEMPTATION.

Historical Romance™   **MEDICAL ROMANCE**™

FREE

4 BOOKS
AND A SURPRISE GIFT!

We would like to take this opportunity to thank you for reading this Mills & Boon® book by offering you the chance to take FOUR more specially selected titles from the Medical Romance™ series absolutely FREE! We're also making this offer to introduce you to the benefits of the Reader Service™—

★ FREE home delivery   ★ FREE gifts and competitions
★ FREE monthly Newsletter   ★ Exclusive Reader Service discounts
★ Books available before they're in the shops

Accepting these FREE books and gift places you under no obligation to buy; you may cancel at any time, even after receiving your free shipment. Simply complete your details below and return the entire page to the address below. *You don't even need a stamp!*

YES! Please send me 4 free Medical Romance books and a surprise gift. I understand that unless you hear from me, I will receive 6 superb new titles every month for just £2.40 each, postage and packing free. I am under no obligation to purchase any books and may cancel my subscription at any time. The free books and gift will be mine to keep in any case.

MOEC

Ms/Mrs/Miss/Mr ....Initials ....
BLOCK CAPITALS PLEASE

Surname ....

Address ....

....

....Postcode ....

Send this whole page to:
UK: FREEPOST CN81, Croydon, CR9 3WZ
EIRE: PO Box 4546, Kilcock, County Kildare (stamp required)

Offer valid in UK and Eire only and not available to current Reader Service subscribers to this series. We reserve the right to refuse an application and applicants must be aged 18 years or over. Only one application per household. Terms and prices subject to change without notice. Offer expires 31st December 2000. As a result of this application, you may receive further offers from Harlequin Mills & Boon Limited and other carefully selected companies. If you would prefer not to share in this opportunity please write to The Data Manager at the address above.

Mills & Boon® is a registered trademark owned by Harlequin Mills & Boon Limited.
Medical Romance™ is being used as a trademark.

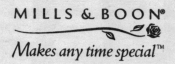